THAT TAKES ME BACK!

ENGAGING SHORT STORIES, FUN TRIVIA AND HIDDEN GEMS FOR SENIORS

Leonard Hamilton

STEP BACK IN TIME AND REAWAKEN CHERISHED MEMORIES!

- ★CAPTIVATING GIFT STORIES
- ★THE BEST PLAYLIST FROM THE 50S TO THE 80S
- ★BEAUTIFUL ICONIC PICTURES FROM THE PAST

Open your phone's camera app and scan the QR Code.

Download Now Your Special Gift!

(Remember to check your e-mail spam folder)

TABLE OF CONTENTS

"Each Era holds its magic, a melody of moments and milestones that compose the symphony of our collective journey."

To those who have lived the melodic ebb and flow of years gone by, and to the generations that follow, who discover and dance to the rhythms of yesteryears...

Introduction

Once Upon a Time in America...

My Epochal Journey

Dear Reader, welcome to a journey that will carry you back through the echoes of time to relive moments that defined eras and shaped generations. As you turn these pages, anticipate a heartfelt reunion with memories, a dance with yesteryears embroidered with tales of triumph, melodies of nostalgia, and narratives that have colored the canvas of our lives.

Each chapter within this book is a time machine crafted to transport you to an age where life was a symphony of simpler joys, profound discoveries, and unforgettable milestones. Imagine the music of the '50s, the harmony, and revolution; each note tells a story, and each rhythm evokes a memory - where were you when the world swayed to these enchanting tunes?

I, too, have lived these moments. I've danced to the iconic tunes, marveled at the cinematic masterpieces, and witnessed the turning tides of history. In these pages, I share the grand narratives and personal anecdotes, the intimate reflections that transform history into a deeply personal, profoundly shared experience.

'That Takes Me Back' is an invitation to traverse memory lanes, revisit the days of old, and experience, once more, the events and emotions that have shaped our lives and our legacies. As you embark on this journey, may every page awaken a memory, ignite a conversation, and revive days gone by with vivid colors and poignant echoes.

Happy reading, and welcome back to the mesmerizing journey of yesteryears!

Chapter 1

Harmony and Nostalgia

Step into a world where every note and frame breathes life into the memorable epochs of history. 'Harmony and Nostalgia' is a timeless journey through the golden eras of music, cinema, and television. Each subsection is a melody, a scene, a moment where art and emotion intertwine, echoing the soul of the times.

From the revolutionary rhythms of the '50s that made hearts dance to the powerful echoes of the '60s that voiced a generation's dreams and rebellions, every tune is a testament to the era's heartbeat. Films weren't merely moving pictures but canvases where each frame painted vivid stories of innovation, revolution, and the human spirit. Television was a magic box unveiling fantastical and profoundly real worlds, illuminating living rooms and imaginations alike.

As you traverse through these pages, you are not just reading but reliving moments where every note, scene, and broadcast was imbued with the essence of an era. A dance with the new rhythms of the '50s, a cinematic journey through the innovative '60s, the diverse sounds of the '70s freedom, and the iconic symphony of the '80s - each a harmonious blend of nostalgia and history.

And because every memory is a treasure, I have sprinkled "Personal Memory Prompts" throughout. Consider these an invitation to dive deeper, to reminisce and reflect. It's not just about the past; it's about reliving the emotions, the excitement, and the experiences that made those years golden. Welcome aboard!

ROCKIN' IN THE 50S

My Dance with New Rhythms

The Night Elvis Walked into My Life

I'll never forget the first time Elvis Presley's voice filled my living room. It was 1956, and I was 13 years old. The old family radio hummed softly in the background on a fantastic evening. Suddenly, the soul-stirring notes of "Heartbreak Hotel" cut through the quiet, and it felt like the universe had stopped just to let this new sound, raw and full of emotion, take center stage.

I was just a teenager back then, and like many of us, I was searching for something - a voice, a sound, an identity that felt like it belonged to us, not our parents. And boy, Elvis was it! With his slick hair, those swiveling hips, and a voice that could make you feel every emotion under the sun, he was the hero we didn't know we were waiting for.

Not everyone knows a fun fact - did you know Elvis's famous black hair was dyed? Yup, he was a natural blonde! And those iconic dance moves? They happened by accident! The first time he gyrated his hips on stage, he was nervous and trying to burn off some energy. Little did he know it would become his signature move!

Elvis was more than just a singer to us; he was a revolution. He was a bit too wild for our parents, a storm of change that threatened the calm waters of the good old days. But for us kids? He was freedom. He was the rebellion we were too scared to voice, the wild, unfiltered expression of a generation who wanted to dance to a different tune. Every performance was our quiet uprising against the old and a loud cheer for the new, the exciting, the now. Elvis wasn't just the King of Rock 'n' Roll; for many of us, he was the king of our revolutions, the beginning of a new chapter where we finally had a say. And looking back, isn't that something extraordinary?

"I'll never forget the first time I heard Elvis Presley. It was 1956, and I was 13. His voice blasted from our family's old radio, and "Heartbreak Hotel" hit me. It was something new, something different. Elvis had this energy, this sound that made you stop and listen.

Back then, all of us kids were looking for something of our own, something that wasn't our parents'. And Elvis, with his wild moves and powerful voice, was it. It's funny thinking back; we didn't just listen to his music - we felt it, lived it.

My parents? They thought Elvis was a bit too wild, but to me, to us, he was freedom. It was like he spoke directly to us and understood what it was like to be young and wanting something more. And even though I was just a kid, I felt part of something bigger that was changing the world in those moments of listening to his music.

Jazz Nights
When Miles and B.B. King Played Our Hearts

I still remember the stories Uncle Robert used to tell us about those jazz-filled nights back in the 50s. Uncle Robert, already in his late thirties during those enchanting nights, loved a good tune and a warm, crowded room where the music wrapped around you like a cozy blanket. One of his favorite stories was about a hidden club in New Orleans, where the air hummed with secrets, and every note told a story.

"You haven't lived until you've heard Miles play live," he'd say with that far-off look in his eyes. Uncle Robert was in the thick of it when Davis' trumpet sang tales of love, loss, and everything in between. It was raw, intimate, like peeking into the soul of the man behind the music. Here is a fun fact: Did you know Miles Davis turned his back to the audience when he played? It wasn't a snub; he got so lost in his music that the whole world melted away.

If Davis was a storm, B.B. King was the calm after. With Lucille, his beloved guitar, in his hands, every strum echoed the heartbeat of a generation looking for their voice. And find it, they did, in the deep, soul-stirring blues that told our stories - the good, the bad, the bittersweet.

Jazz and blues were more than music to us; they were like close pals sharing our journey, echoing our laughter, tears, and triumphs. These rhythms didn't just live in smoky clubs or on the radio waves; they pulsed through our veins, a testament to a time when every note and lyric was a piece of our collective soul.

And you know what's magic? Those tunes laid the golden bricks for the paths that rock, hip-hop, and R&B would boldly tread. They were the unsung heroes of our narrative, a melody-laden bridge from the silent yesteryears to the loud, unapologetic tomorrows.

So, when I think back to those stories Uncle Robert used to tell, it isn't just the music I remember; it's the unity, the shared spirit that jazz and blues kindled in us all. In these sweet reminisces, amidst the echo of notes long played, we find not just the soul of an era but the undying spirit of us - the silent dancers to the timeless tunes of jazz and blues.

Harmonies Under the Starlit Sky

The Melodies that Danced with Our Souls

Every time I hear a doo-wop tune, it's like a time machine whooshing me back to those warm, starry nights when the air was thick with dreams and the songs of The Platters and The Drifters were our companions. There was something almost magical about those melodies; they had the power to make the whole world fade away, leaving nothing but the harmonious chorus of voices that seemed to echo the heartbeat of our generation.

I can still feel the buzz of those Saturday nights when we'd gather around the old jukebox at the corner diner. Each of us had that one song, the tune that felt like it was written just for us. And when "Only You" by The Platters floated through the air, every worry and doubt disappeared. Did you know that song was initially rejected by producers? But, oh, when it hit the airwaves, it was like the universe hummed along!

Doo-wop and R&B weren't just genres but the rhythms of our lives, loves, and losses. It's fascinating. How a simple tune can encapsulate a moment, an era, a feeling and lock it away, ready to be unfurled with every listen. Those harmonious tunes were the seeds from which the mighty trees of soul, funk, and contemporary R&B grew. Every note is a branch reaching out through the decades, linking our simple, starry nights to today's dazzling, complex world.

Whenever the city lights glow too bright, and the world spins too fast, I find my sanctuary in those hauntingly beautiful melodies. In the silky notes of doo-wop and the soul-stirring tunes of R&B, I see a bridge to those simpler times, a reminder of the starlit nights where dreams were as boundless as the melodies that danced under the open sky.

When the World Rocked and Rolled

Rebels with a Tune

Do you remember those heady days when rock 'n' roll burst onto the scene like a wild, untamable spirit that took hold of us all? Man, those were the days! I remember the first time I heard 'Roll Over Beethoven' by Chuck Berry. I was sitting on the porch steps, the radio beside me barely catching the station. Every strum was like a jolt of electricity. I felt seen and heard – it was the language of our quiet rebellion, the anthem for every one of us kids who felt the world hadn't quite gotten us yet.

Now, Elvis was the King, no doubt about it. But let me tell you about the unsung heroes, the rock wizards who strummed the soundtrack to our coming of age. Chuck Berry with his wild riffs, Jerry Lee Lewis setting the piano on fire (not figuratively – the man legit set his piano ablaze!), and Little Richard, oh sweet Richard, who could make you feel every emotion under the sun in a three-minute tune.

One of my sweetest memories? It's got to be that summer evening, a sky painted with hues of orange and purple, friends all around, and Chuck

Berry's "Johnny B. Goode" echoing in the air. We didn't just hear the music; we felt it, every note, every beat in the very core of our souls. And oh, did you know Chuck initially titled the song "Ida May" but changed it? Yeah, it's just one of those golden nuggets from the golden age of music!

Rock 'n' roll wasn't just music but a revolution. Suddenly, we weren't just kids; we were rockers, rebels with a cause and a tune. Our jeans got tighter, our hair longer, and every lyric and rhythm echoed the unspoken dreams, fears, and defiant hope of a generation caught between the old world's constraints and the uncharted waters of a future we were yet to write.

When I look back, it's with a heart brimming with gratitude. Because, you see, rock 'n' roll gave us more than iconic tunes and legendary artists; it gifted us a voice, a space to be heard, seen, and celebrated in all our wild, untamed, and unapologetic glory. In those electric nights, amidst the strums and beats of a world rocking and rolling, we found the tunes and the timeless echoes of our untold stories.

Twang and Heartstrings
The Ballads that Colored Our World

Isn't it funny how specific sounds and certain melodies can whisk you away to another time and place? Every time I hear the smooth, soulful twangs of country tunes, I'm back to those tender years when Johnny Cash and Patsy Cline weren't just artists; they were storytellers weaving the tales of our lives with every lyric, every note.

I'll never forget those stories my older brother Mike, who was in his early twenties, used to tell. His eyes would light up with the energy of a live wire as he'd transport us to those magical nights at the Grand Ole Opry. Mike, barely out of his teens with the spirit of adventure coursing through his veins, was not just an observer but a participant in those iconic evenings. It was more than a show; it was an experience, a communion of souls bound together by the heart-tugging chords of country music. Though a young man, Mike spoke with a reverence that belied his years, every recollection etched with the fine lines of profound memories.

Speaking of Mr. Cash, did you know that his iconic song "A Boy Named Sue" was penned by none other than the legendary Shel Silverstein? The same genius behind those whimsical poems that danced through our childhood also crafted the ballad of that unforgettable face-off at San Quentin.

Now, while Johnny was the "Man in Black," let's not forget the radiant Patsy Cline. She was the kind of artist who didn't just sing; she poured her soul into every word. Tunes like "Crazy" and "Walkin' After Midnight" weren't just songs; they were anthems for every soul that ever loved, lost, and found the courage to love again.

Mike's enthusiasm when he spoke of the Grand Ole Opry made it a living entity in our young imaginations. Through his eyes, we saw the stage where legends were born and felt the soulful twangs of country music as they reached out, weaving through the mountains and prairies to touch the hearts of folks from all walks of life.

So, in those quiet moments when the hustle and bustle of today's world gets a little too loud, I close my eyes and let those cherished tunes, those soul-stirring ballads, as vividly narrated by my brother Mike, take me back to a time when the world was a melody, and every heartbeat, a note in the beautiful, soulful symphony of country music's golden age.

Heartthrobs and Hit Tunes

The Days We Screamed and Swooned

Oh, my stars! Do you remember those butterfly-in-the-stomach moments whenever Frankie Avalon hit the high notes? We were just kids, but we knew a heartthrob when we saw one! And Paul Anka? Come on, "Put Your Head on My Shoulder" was the anthem of every school dance and moonlit walk home.

One of my favorite snippets from those days is of my younger sister, Annie. One evening, the golden voice of Paul Anka floated from the radio, and she just froze, a spoonful of mashed potatoes mid-air, her eyes wide and dreamy. The family watched in amused silence as she swayed gently, utterly entranced. At that moment, Anka wasn't just in our living room; he was serenading Annie amidst a sea of stars!

Did you know Anka was just 16 when he penned "Diana"? Yeah, a kid weaving magic that made the whole world swoon!

But wait, it wasn't just about the music. It was an era where every new single drop meant crowded record stores and radios turned up to the max. We didn't just listen to songs; we devoured each melody and lyric etching into our hearts, birthing an adoration beyond posters on the wall. Fan clubs sprouted like wildflowers, and every issue of "16 Magazine" wasn't just pages but holy scriptures detailing the sacred lives of our idols.

And there we were, amidst it all - a generation not just witnessing but living the rise of a culture that would transcend time. Those tunes, those idols, they weren't just passing phases. They were bookmarks, etching indelible marks into the narrative of our youth, echoes of an era where every beat, every melody was a hushed whisper of rebellion, love, and the unutterable magic of being young.

SOUNDS OF THE 60S

My Echoes of a Dynamic Era

When The Beatles Crossed the Pond

Who could forget the first time we heard "I Want to Hold Your Hand"? I remember it like it was yesterday - the crackle of the radio, the anticipation in the air, and then those iconic chords blaring out, taking not just me but the whole nation by storm. It wasn't just music; it was a movement. The Beatles had landed, and America was about to get its first taste of Beatlemania!

My cousin Jimmy and I were glued to the black-and-white TV set when The Beatles made their legendary appearance on The Ed Sullivan Show. Over 73 million people tuned in that night! It felt like the entire country held its breath as John, Paul, George, and Ringo rocked our world with their catchy tunes and signature mop-top haircuts.

Every corner you turned, there was Beatles fever. Lunchboxes, T-shirts, posters - you name it. The Beatles weren't just on our radios; they were in our homes, conversations, and hearts.

Did you know the Beatles sold over 1.6 billion singles in the U.S. alone? Or that the term "Beatlemania" was coined by the British press and quickly adopted worldwide to describe the state of frenzied fans? It wasn't just a craze; it was a global phenomenon. It felt like the world spun on the axis of their records.

The Fab Four weren't just musicians - they were magicians, weaving a spell that united us all in a world of melodies, hope, and unbridled joy. To this day, when I hear the opening chords of "Hey Jude," it's like stepping into a time capsule where every note and every lyric is a cherished brushstroke in the colorful canvas of our golden years. Ah, those were the days!

Blowin' in the Wind
The Echo of a Generation

I still remember the evening air, tinged with the scent of summer blossoms and the distant murmur of a restless world. Amid the hum of life's complexity, there was a voice, clear as a bell, echoing the questions we all held deep within our souls. That voice belonged to none other than Bob Dylan.

One evening, as I sat with friends - a mix of dreamers and doubters, believers and seekers - someone pulled out a record, the grooves rich with the poetry that would define our era. The needle dropped, and Dylan's voice filled the room, "How many roads must a man walk down..." Every word and every note was a revelation.

Bob Dylan wasn't just a singer; he was a poet, a prophet of sorts, painting pictures with his lyrics that held up a mirror to the world we knew and the changes that swirled around us. We were on the cusp of something profound, and Dylan was the troubadour who sang our collective soul's journey.

Have you ever heard the tale of Dylan going electric at the Newport Folk Festival in 1965? Oh, the uproar it caused! Folk purists viewed it as a betrayal, while others, like me, saw it as an artist evolving, the electric chords striking the tune of a changing world.

As the '60s unfolded, with its triumphs and tribulations, there was Bob, with his harmonica and distinctive voice, echoing the highs and lows, the hopes, and the despairs. His songs were our companions; a solace and rallying cry rolled into one. We weren't just listeners but participants in a lyrical dance that would shape future generations.

Woodstock

A Sea of Souls and Songs

I wasn't one of the half a million souls that converged upon that dairy farm in the Catskills back in '69, but my younger cousin Johnny, who was in his late teens at the time, was. Brimming with the indomitable spirit of youth and the fiery zeal of a generation echoing change, Johnny ventured where I did not. Oh, how I remember the enthusiasm in his eyes, the exhilaration in his voice, painting every detail. Each word and each recall was like a living echo of Jimi Hendrix's guitar, and the enthralled audience hung onto every note.

"Half a million," Johnny would say, shaking his head in bewilderment, "and not a trace of violence. Can you believe that?" Every recount was drenched in the mystique of an era where peace, love, and music weren't just words but were alive, dancing in every breath and heartbeat.

Did you know that Woodstock wasn't meant to be free? Tickets were sold, but as the sea of humanity swelled, the fences and the notion of restriction and possession came crumbling down. It was a revelation, not of anarchy, but of a collective spirit that soared beyond the mundane, breathing in the air of liberty and exhaling melodies of transcendence.

"I heard Hendrix play the 'Star-Spangled Banner,'" Johnny reminisced one day, his eyes distant yet bright as if each note had left an indelible imprint on his soul. It wasn't a rendition but a revelation weaving the tumultuous sentiments of an era – a nation at war, a youth in rebellion, and a society on the cusp of transformation.

Though I didn't tread the muddy grounds of Woodstock, every recount from Johnny, every echo of that enchanted melody, transported me to a world where music was a sanctuary, and every chord, a hymn of a generation's unyielding spirit. Each story is a vacation back to three days where time stood still, and music, oh sweet music, painted the dawn with strokes of freedom, rebellion, and unity.

Harmony in Detroit
When Motown Was Our Anthem

During the turbulence and transformative energy of the '60s, we all found a melodious sanctuary in Motown. No, I never strolled down West Grand Boulevard in Detroit, but who needed to when you had that magical Motown sound, each record a passport, transporting every listener straight to Hitsville?

I remember Sundays at Aunt Lisa's, where the air was thick with the aroma of her famous pot roast and the spirited harmonies of The Supremes. "Stop! In the Name of Love," they'd command, and like clockwork, we'd freeze, hands outstretched, utterly captivated. Aunt Lisa wasn't just a fan; in her heart, she was the fourth member of The Supremes.

Did you know Motown had a charm that even mesmerized The Beatles? Oh, yes! They were fans, too, covering tracks from the label's legendary lineup. Motown was more than a sound; it was a unifying, soul-stirring echo that danced across continents, breaking barriers and weaving hearts harmoniously.

Marvin Gaye was another story, a voice that could soothe the storms, incite a rebellion, and summon love with a mere whisper. I hadn't known soul until "I Heard It Through the Grapevine" spun on my turntable for the first time. It wasn't just a song but a narrative of passion, betrayal, and the raw, unuttered emotions that dwell in the silent spaces between us.

Though the golden Motown sign was miles away, its resonance lived in our living room, in every gathering, every celebration, every quiet night where solace was found in the velvety caress of those iconic tunes. In an era of change, Motown was our constant, a melodic embrace where soul, pop, and R&B weren't just genres but the language of our unspoken souls.

Kaleidoscope Sounds

The Psychedelic Wave

I'll admit, the '60s was a mixed bag of tunes for me. Elvis had my heart, and Motown got my soul, but psychedelic rock? That was the wild child of music I watched from a distance, equally wary and fascinated.

I can still recall the first eerie yet mesmerizing notes of The Doors' "Light My Fire" crackling through my neighbor's garage. Benny, a mop-haired teen with an insatiable appetite for the offbeat, had his hands full of records with vibrant, otherworldly cover art. "It's an experience, not just music," Benny would say, his eyes wide with the thrill of the new sound wave sweeping the youth off their feet.

Now, I wasn't one to dabble in the hallucinogenic fervor that defined the era. Still, Lord knows, you didn't need to drop acid to be swept into the hypnotic melodies of the Grateful Dead. Their music was a trip, an auditory odyssey that made the ordinary world morph and melt into something... more.

Did you know that "psychedelic" derives from two Greek words meaning "soul-manifesting"? Considering how these bands manifested a realm where music and mind-melded, it is a fitting term. The Doors, Grateful Dead, and Jefferson Airplane weren't just bands but conjurers of a soundscape where every note was a door flung open to the endless corridors of perception.

Amid the moon landings and civil rights marches, psychedelic rock weaved its colorful threads into the rich tapestry of the '60s. It was the echo of an era where barriers broke, minds expanded, and music wasn't just heard but profoundly, irrevocably felt. Even from the sidelines, as an observer rather than a participant, the vibrational pull of that psychedelic symphony was undeniable, an undercurrent that hummed in the bones of a generation eager to explore beyond the seen into the untamable terrains of the unseen.

Stones Vibes
The Rebellious Echo in Our Ears

In 1964, at 21, life was a mix of uncertainties and exhilarating freedoms. The Beatles had already whispered the tunes of change, but when The Rolling Stones exploded onto the scene, it felt like a storm after the calm.

I was a young adult, teetering on the edge of the rest of my life, and the Stones were the defiant shout into the void of silent expectations.

One evening, a college classmate pulled me into his dorm, his eyes glittering with the thrill of the secret he was about to share. The room was cramped, adorned with the predictable rebellion of youth. Amidst this, he unveiled an LP with a dramatic flourish. "The Rolling Stones," he announced. Every note of "(I Can't Get No) Satisfaction" was more than a song; it was a catharsis, echoing the silent screams of our generation's restless spirit.

Though we were stepping into the roles of adults, inside, a rebellious child lived, breathed, and sang along to every lyric Mick Jagger belted. The Stones weren't just music. They were a rebellion, an echoing sentiment that we weren't alone in this tumultuous journey from childhood restraints to adulthood's freedoms and fears.

And here's something not everyone knows - the Stones were dubbed the anti-Beatles. They were raw, unfiltered, wild in a world of poised decorum. Every concert was a sanctuary where that inner child, fearless and untamable, danced freely to the rhythmic beats of insurmountable life echoing in every corner of the hall.

70S FREEDOM

My Dawns of Diverse Sounds

Disco Fever

The Night the Stars Danced

If there's one thing that can instantly transport me back to the spirited '70s, it's the hypnotic pulse of disco music that danced in the air and lured us all to the dance floor. I was in my 30s, and although I wasn't a teenager anymore, who could resist the call of those hypnotic rhythms and the glittering embrace of the disco ball?

I remember the anticipation of Saturday nights when the neon lights seemed to shimmer slightly brighter, and the city's energy hummed with an uncontainable vibrancy. My buddies and I weren't the 'suits' then. We were the kings and queens of the night, our spirits as wild and uncontainable as the curly locks that bounced freely on our shoulders.

I recall one particular night – oh, what a night it was! The air was thick with the electrifying beats of Donna Summer's "I Feel Love." Every note was a spell, every lyric a siren's call, beckoning us closer to a world where the intoxicating symphony of freedom and youth drowned out the worries of mortgages and office desks.

There were no cell phones, no incessant pings of emails waiting to be answered. It was just us and the music. The Bee Gees weren't just voices on a record; they were the narrators of our lives, and "Stayin' Alive" was more than a song - it was an anthem, a celebration of the vitality and exuberance that coursed unabatedly through our veins.

And here's a nugget that might tickle your fancy: Remember "Soul Train"? That show was the golden ticket for any disco enthusiast. It wasn't just a dance show; it was a cultural icon, a platform that brought the pulsating heart of the disco era into our living rooms. Artists we now revere as legends were once fresh faces on that stage, their melodies weaving the soundtrack of a decade marked by liberation, expression, and an unyielding thirst for life.

So, while the times have changed, the wild pulse of those unforgettable nights has simmered to the gentle rhythm of reminiscence. Now and then, when the moon is just right, and the stars align, you might catch me, a smile on my face, my soul swaying to the immortal rhythm of a time when the stars didn't just shine - they danced.

Rock Legends

Echoes of Thunderous Applause and Electric Air

Rock music in the late '70s wasn't just music; it was a visceral experience, a rhapsody of freedom that roared in our veins and echoed the rebellious symphony of a generation. By the time bands like Led Zeppelin and Pink Floyd became my companions in the stillness of the night, I was in my mid-30s. The world had seen a decade of rapid change, and so had I.

I remember the first time the eerie yet beautiful chords of Led Zeppelin's "Stairway to Heaven" graced my ears. I was 35, more seasoned by life's triumphs and trials, yet still as enchanted by the power of music as I was in my youthful days. It was a melody from another world, a fusion of poetry and soul that transcended the mundane and ordinary. My friends and I would gather, the vinyl record spinning, the needle dancing delicately to the timeless tunes. Each note was an exploration, a journey to the mystic lands where legends were born, and immortality was a song away.

And then there was Pink Floyd. Oh, the psychedelic, immersive universe of "The Dark Side of the Moon." It was more than music; it was art, a masterpiece painted with the celestial brushstrokes of talent and genius. We'd lose ourselves in the cosmic echoes, every chord a stardust trail leading to the enigmatic beyond.

In this golden era of rock, I was not just an observer but a participant. Every concert and every new album release marks the chapters of my journey amidst the backdrop of a world in transformation.

Speaking of cosmic, here's a piece of trivia for you. Did you ever wonder where the haunting, enigmatic allure of Pink Floyd's "The Wall" stemmed from? It was born from the ashes of disillusionment, a testament to the band's tumultuous dance with fame. Every note and lyric was a fragment of a soul seeking solace amidst the turbulent tides of adoration and isolation.

And amidst this mosaic of soul-stirring melodies, Queen stood as the epitome of anthemic rock. "We Will Rock You" wasn't just a song; it was a clarion call, a unifying anthem that echoed the unyielding spirit of a generation unwilling to be tamed. In the echo of every stomp and clap, in the resonance of Freddie Mercury's immortal voice, we found our battle cry, our song of freedom.

Country Outlaws

Rebels, Roads, and Rhythms

There's something about country music's raw, unfiltered soul that no other genre can replicate. In my early 30s, the transformation from the carefree days of youth to the responsibilities of adulthood made the resonating anthems of rebellion and freedom all the more poignant. It's like whisky for the ears, and back in the '70s, a couple of outlaws made sure it hit hard and left you with that warm, burning sensation of living life unchained.

I wasn't one to frequent the honky-tonks, but I had a good friend, Jack, a die-hard fan of the Outlaw Country movement. Jack was as wild as they came, an untethered soul, much like the artists he adored. I can still recall him, a constant figure in the local bars, his voice drowned but spirit unyielding amidst the blare of Johnny Cash and Willie Nelson.

One evening, Jack dragged me to one of those smoky old joints. The air was thick with anticipation, and then there it was - the gravelly voice of Johnny Cash echoing through the room, singing "Hurt." It was raw, gritty - a voice that had lived, lost and battled through every note. That night, even a rock 'n' roll loyalist like me had to admit there was an undeniable power in those lyrics, a soul-stirring magic that transcended musical loyalties.

Willie Nelson was Jack's other muse. I didn't need to attend a concert to understand Willie's distinct sound. Jack's renditions of "On the Road Again" were loud, slightly off-key, but filled with a passion to which even Willie would've tipped his hat.

And here's a nugget for you – did you know Willie Nelson and Waylon

Jennings were the cornerstones of the "Outlaw Country" movement? They were the rebels who looked at the polished sound coming out of Nashville and said, "Not for us." They sought the dusty, raw roots of country, a sound that was as untamed as the landscapes they sang about.

Whenever I hear the rugged tunes of "outlaw country," I'm instantly transported back to those days. It was a time of rebellion, a time when a new breed of country music, unfiltered and unabashed, echoed the unyielding spirit of folks like Jack – folks who lived life with the throttle wide open, where music was the soul's rebellion and every note a manifesto of freedom.

Punk Rock

When the Streets Sang the Rebellion

Punk rock was the kind of uproar I initially steered clear of. Raw, unbridled energy lurked in the dazzling disco lights and the majestic riffs of rock giants - too stark, too rebellious, even for our tumultuous times. I was born in '43, and my ears were tuned to the melodies of the past. Still, my nephew Danny was a stark contrast, a wild spirit, and the epitome of the punk rock generation.

Danny was a spectacle with his ripped jeans, leather jacket adorned with pins of The Ramones and The Clash, and an unruly mop of hair that danced to the rhythm of rebellion. His world was a far cry from mine. Where I sought solace and nostalgia, he sought the uproar and the revolution. A revolution resounded in the underground clubs and spilled onto the gritty streets.

I ventured into Danny's tumultuous world one night out of sheer curiosity. The underground scene was alive with a pulsating energy, a raw echo of revolt. The Ramones' unfiltered sound and disregard for the polished notes hit the air with a piercing intensity. It wasn't the melody but the message that held you captive. Every strum and every beat was a stark declaration of rebellion, an anthem for the unheard.

Here's a slice of trivia that Danny once rattled off - did you know the term "punk rock" wasn't the brainchild of these rebellious souls but was coined by American rock critics in the early 70s? It was meant for the 60s garage rock bands and the subsequent acts that carried the baton of their unrefined, unruly legacy.

I was a visitor in punk rock, an outsider peeping into an era of unapologetic revolt. It was raw, loud, and bore no semblance to the harmonious tunes that once graced my record player. Yet, every strum, every rebellious lyric echoed the sentiment of a generation seeking to carve out their space in a world where the norms were as fluctuating as the tunes that hit the airwaves. Even today, the raw notes of The Clash's "London Calling" reverberate, a stark reminder of the era when the streets sang the rebellion, unfiltered and unyielding.

Singer-Songwriters
When Melodies Told Stories

I've always had a soft spot for melodies that tell stories, where every note is steeped in raw emotion, and every lyric paints a vivid portrait. It was during the '70s that these musical narrators emerged, capturing the complexity of human experiences in their soulful tunes. Each song became a canvas where emotions, stories, and cultures converged, offering listeners a harmonious journey through diverse human backgrounds.

Though I was a child of the earlier era, there was no resisting the intimate embrace of James Taylor's melodies and Joni Mitchell's poignant lyrics. It wasn't a first-hand experience, but my sister Alice brought these ethereal experiences to life for me. Alice was a free spirit of the 70s; her soul swayed with the tender ballads, and her eyes gleamed with the reflection of the moonlit serenades.

Alice used to narrate, "James isn't just a singer. He's a storyteller. When he sings, it's like he unveils a chapter of his soul, and you can't help but walk the journey with him." She was particularly fond of "Fire and Rain." To her, it wasn't just a song but a haunting narrative, a soul bared open, raw, and unfiltered.

And who could overlook the grace of Joni Mitchell? Her intricate and profound lyrics were like a painter's brushstrokes, crafting landscapes imbued with emotions and tales untold. With her expressive eyes, Alice would get lost in the echoing notes of "Big Yellow Taxi," as if every word resonated with a chapter of her existence.

A slice of trivia that has always stuck with me – did you know Carole King's album "Tapestry" was not just a musical but a cultural sensation? It swept the Grammys in 1972 and marked its territory on the charts for six years. Alice's vinyl collection boasted a well-worn copy, the grooves bearing testament to the countless evenings spent in the soulful embrace of Carole's melodies.

In the universe of dissonant melodies and roaring anthems, the singer-songwriters of the '70s were the quiet echoes of introspection. Their tunes weren't born from the clamor but from the silent recesses of the soul, where stories lay waiting to be unveiled, one haunting melody at a time. Alice might have been the first-hand witness, but the repercussions of those soulful narratives transcend time, echoing the untainted, unspoken symphony of the human experience.

Groovin' with the Greats

A Funkadelic Journey

As much as I found solace in the tender melodies of singer-songwriters and the fierce rebellion of rock, there was this whole other world of rhythm and soul that was just electric. Funk was a musical jolt to the system. While I might have been too stodgy to immerse myself in the scene, my younger cousin Tony was living and breathing the golden age of funk.

"Man, you haven't lived until you've felt the room quake with James Brown's beats," Tony would tell me, his eyes wide, his soul resonating with the live performance's energy. He was there, amidst the ecstatic crowd, when "Get Up Offa That Thing" first blared through the speakers, a powerful command that had every body moving, every soul grooving.

With his Afro as grand and bold as his spirit, Tony was our family's gateway to this vibrant world. He'd spin tales of the enigmatic George Clinton and his Parliament-Funkadelic ensemble. I might not have been front and center at those concerts. Still, through Tony's vivid recounts, I could almost feel the eclectic, pulsating rhythms, a surreal blend of soul, jazz, and R&B that refused to be boxed in by labels or norms.

A little nugget that Tony once shared - and it stuck with me, likely because it was just as quirky as him - was about those iconic bass lines. Can you believe they often belted out those rich, thumping notes from a keyboard, not a bass guitar? Yep, synthesizers like the Moog were the unsung heroes, injecting that unmistakable sonic flair that defined funk.

I was a spectator to the funk revolution, witnessing it through Tony's exhilarated eyes. But even from the sidelines, it was clear – funk wasn't just music. It was an unbridled celebration of freedom, innovation, and the sheer, unapologetic joy of losing yourself to rhythms that pulsated through your veins, etched into your soul, and lingered long after the music faded. Every recount of Tony's funk-infused escapades is a reminder - the '70s might have been a time of change and challenges, but we danced through it all!

Rock Giants

The Spectacle and Roar of Arena Icons

Arena rock, oh, how that brings back vivid images of electrified crowds, guitar riffs that echoed into the night, and performances that were larger than life. In the '70s, bands like Aerosmith and KISS weren't just heard; they were an experience, a storm of sound and visuals that swept you away.

My colleague Tom, a spirited soul, always a bit more rebellious, snuck into a KISS concert one crisp fall evening. Tom was younger, and the energy of youth radiated from him, always ready to dive headfirst into the thrills of life. The increasing demands of adulthood anchored me, but Tom... Tom was free.

"Man, you should've seen it!" He'd recount, eyes wide, animated, as if the echoes of the music still resonated in his bones. "The entire stadium was alive, pulsating with energy. Every strum, every beat, it was like a collective heartbeat."

With their iconic painted faces and theatrical performances, KISS was the epitome of this musical and visual explosion. The pyrotechnics and the elaborate stage setups transformed music into an all-encompassing experience. It was a rebellion, a liberation, a communal dance of individuals unshackled.

Did you know KISS took theatrics to another level? Fire breathing, blood-spitting, and smoking guitars were all part of the spectacle. Every concert was an unspoken pact of wild, uncontainable freedom. In this ephemeral world, the rules of the mundane were suspended, and in those moments, we were immortal.

I didn't witness it firsthand, but through Tom's exuberant recounts, I lived those concerts and felt the repercussions, the collective euphoria. The '70s was a time when music wasn't just heard but viscerally felt: every beat, every note, a rebellion, a declaration, a collective dance of untethered souls.

Rhythms of Resistance

When Reggae Touched the World

I can still recall the first time the soul-stirring reggae rhythms flowed through my ears. It was 1975, and the air was thick with the buzz of a changing world. One evening, as I was perusing the record store, I saw an unassuming album with a vibrant cover – Bob Marley's "Live!"

The needle dropped, and so did the world around me. Those penetrating lyrics and captivating rhythms weren't just sounds but echoes of a struggle, a passionate plea for unity and love amidst a world of division and hatred. Marley's raw emotion in "No Woman, No Cry" wasn't something you'd hear; you'd feel it deep in your bones, weaving through your soul, connecting you to millions around the globe.

I've read somewhere that Bob Marley never wrote down his lyrics; they flowed from his soul, pure and unfiltered, just like his message of love and unity. Each chord and word was a piece of his journey, an insight into the depths of his wisdom.

And here is some trivia for the road: did you know that Bob Marley's "Legend," which beautifully encapsulated his iconic sounds, became the best-selling reggae album of all time? And here's a nugget - it hit the shelves three years after Marley took his leave. Now, that's the power of music; it crosses borders, transcends time, and lingers, evergreen, in the annals of history, just like the sweet, enduring strains of "One Love" that still play in the corners of my mind.

THE 80S SYMPHONY

My Era of Icons

Moonwalk Memories

The Night Michael Jackson Made History

In the golden '80s, my kids were the right age to get swept up in the frenzy of pop culture. I'll never forget the Saturday evening when my daughter, all pigtails and wide-eyed wonder, pulled me into the living room. "Daddy, you've got to see this," she'd chirped. On our wooden-cased television was a young man with an electrifying presence, dazzling the world. Michael Jackson, the King of Pop, unveiled "Thriller" to an awe-struck world.

I remember thinking, "This isn't just a song; it's a cinematic masterpiece." My daughter was entranced as she beat the rhythm with her hands. At that moment, Jackson wasn't just on TV – he was in our living room, a mesmerizing blend of music and magic that transcended the ordinary and made every viewer feel like a guest in his world of wonder.

Did you know Michael's red jacket in the "Thriller" video became so iconic that it's been displayed in museums? And here's another gem - "Thriller" wasn't just an album but an experience. Released in 1982, it became the world's best-selling album, a testament to Jackson's unique ability to fuse pop, rock, and soul into something universally adored.

I'll admit I wasn't much for pop music back then. Still, I witnessed the Michael Jackson era through my daughter's eyes. Music, dance, and spectacle blended into something utterly unforgettable at this time. Every spin, every moonwalk step, was more than dance - it was art in motion. This era-defining masterpiece echoed the audacity and creativity of a generation unafraid to redefine the norms.

MTV Mania
When Screens Brought Songs to Life

Back in my day, we listened to tunes on the radio, vinyl records spinning magic in our living rooms. But in the '80s, oh boy, did that change. My son, a teenager then with wild hair and an insatiable appetite for all things new, was the one who introduced me to it - MTV. I remember squinting at the screen one evening, a blend of curiosity and bemusement, as The Buggles claimed that 'Video Killed the Radio Star.' It was the dawn of a new era.

Did you know MTV aired for the first time on August 1, 1981, and that song by The Buggles was the first music video to grace the channel?

MTV became not just a broadcaster but a cultural phenomenon that defined a generation.

To me, a guy who grew up with the crackling intimacy of radio, this was an alien world. Yet, there was something irresistible about it. Watching David Bowie or Madonna on screen, their music complemented by vivid imagery was like opening a window to their souls. Music wasn't just for the ears anymore; it was a visual, visceral experience that appealed to every sense.

I remember gatherings where we'd all huddle around the TV - the neighbors, family, the kids, and their friends - eyes comprehensive as Michael Jackson defied gravity with his moonwalk. These were moments of communal awe, glued together by the mesmerizing allure of MTV.

As much as I was a man molded by the harmonious melodies of the '50s and '60s, I couldn't help but get swept into this new tidal wave of musical expression. It was different and audacious, and whether you were a fan of rock, pop, or something in between, MTV had something for you. It was the ultimate democratization of music, making stars out of the unknown and bringing the iconic into our living rooms with a revolutionary vibrancy and immediacy.

When the World Sang Together
A Glimpse into Live Aid

Now, I've seen my fair share of concerts and festivals, but nothing, and I mean nothing, could have prepared me for the spectacle that was Live Aid. It wasn't something I attended - oh, I was past those days of standing in a sea of jubilant, swaying bodies, though the charm never truly fades. No, I watched it from my cozy living room, a cup of hot coffee in hand, and the infectious energy still managed to seep through the television screen.

Did you know that Live Aid was one of the largest-scale satellite link-ups and television broadcasts of all time? An estimated 1.9 billion viewers across 150 nations tuned in live.

I recall my niece, an energetic soul with a love for all things musical, raving about it. She had managed to snag tickets, a feat in itself, and her excitement was palpable even over the phone. "Uncle, it's not just a concert; it's history in the making," she'd told me. Every call after was a countdown, her voice brimming with anticipation.

On July 13, 1985, the world did pause. The best of the best graced the stage - Queen, U2, David Bowie, to name a few. Music wasn't just music that day but a universal language, a global anthem of unity echoing from London's Wembley Stadium to Philadelphia's John F. Kennedy Stadium. We weren't just audiences; we were witnesses to something intangible.

I remember the silence before Bob Geldof took the stage, the hush of millions as if the earth was holding its breath. And then, the music flowed, and it was as if barriers dissolved. There was no you or I, no countries or borders; there was humanity dancing to the rhythm of hope in all its flawed, beautiful splendor.

I wasn't there, but I was a part of it, as we all were. We touched something greater amid those fleeting moments' harmonious clash of chords and lyrics. Live Aid wasn't just a concert. It was proof that music could bridge divides and, for a brief, glorious moment, make us one.

Beats of the Street

The Rise of Hip-Hop

Hip-hop was a genre I admittedly took a while to warm up to. It was a symphony of the streets, raw, unabashed, and pulsating with the heartbeat of a restless, vibrant youth. My nephew Alex, a Brooklyn native with an ear forever pressed to the ground of the latest trends, was the one who pulled me into this world feet first.

Did you know Def Jam Recordings was initially started in Rick Rubin's dormitory at New York University?

I remember one afternoon, Alex barged into my living room, a cassette tape clutched in his hands like a treasure. "Uncle," he'd said, eyes wide and gleaming, "this ain't just music; it's poetry, a movement!" And before I could respond, the room was filled with Run-DMC's rhythmic beats and potent lyrics. Their music wasn't just heard; it was felt, each word a pulse, each beat a step closer to an unseen, unspoken revolution.

And there, amidst my well-kept living room with the old records lining the shelves, a bridge between generations was built. Hip-hop wasn't my music, but it was Alex's, and through his eyes, I saw a world where words wielded power, where music was a vehicle of change.

It wasn't long before names like LL Cool J, Grandmaster Flash, and the iconic Def Jam Recordings became familiar echoes in conversations. Witnessing the dawn of hip-hop was observing an evolution, a new chapter in the storied legacy of music. Hip-hop had marked its territory from the graffiti-strewn walls of the Bronx to the glitzy award show stages.

It was a narrative of resilience, an anthem of a generation carving out their space in the world. And though my feet were firmly planted in the tunes of yesteryears, I couldn't help but admire the tenacity, the fiery spirit of rebellion and innovation that hip-hop epitomized. Through Alex's impassioned explanations and the hypnotic beats that now often filled my home, I came not just to hear but to listen. In the symphony of the streets, amidst the rap and rhythm, I found an echo of the timeless dance between rebellion and art.

Rockstars and Rebels

The Unleashed Symphony of Glam Metal

Back in the day, Mötley Crüe, Bon Jovi, and Guns N' Roses weren't just bands; they were explosions of sound and color in a world that was starting to feel a little grey around the edges. My colleagues and I were rooted in the classics, yet here was a sound that was as loud as it was defiant, anthems that wouldn't let you sit and listen – they demanded you stand up and scream.

I remember the neighbor's kid, Brian, with his long hair and leather jackets, blaring 'Sweet Child o' Mine' from his beat-up car. Every chord was a rebellion; every lyric screamed freedom from the young, wild, and free generation. It wasn't my cup of tea, honestly. I'd sometimes shake my head and chuckle – the extravagance, the glitz, it was a world apart. But, oh, how those tunes would stick in your head! They weren't just songs but anthems of a new age, a testament to the ever-changing, ever-thrilling world of music. And did you know Mötley Crüe's drummer, Tommy Lee, had his drum set mounted on a roller coaster track, so he'd loop upside down while playing during their live shows?

Talk about taking performances to new heights!

Synthetic Harmonies
The Dawn of a New Sonic Age

A new wave of sound carved its niche in the eclectic landscape of the '80s music scene. It wasn't the raging power chords of glam metal or the poignant narratives of singer-songwriters, but a genre gleaming with the futuristic shimmer of synthesizers: the iconic Synth-Pop. I was an old soul, born in the robust rhythms of rock 'n' roll and the soul-stirring melodies of the '60s. But who could ignore the infectious beats of Depeche Mode's "Just Can't Get Enough" or the eerie, mesmerizing harmonies of The Human League's "Don't You Want Me?"

My niece, Sarah, a teenager with wild curls and an insatiable appetite for all things modern, 'd introduce me to this enigmatic world. The family gathered for a barbecue one summer evening, and Sarah took command of the stereo. The music that ensued was unfamiliar, filled with electronic beats and artificial sounds I had never encountered before.

Yet, there was a method to this electronic madness, a rhythm that made your feet tap and your soul dance. It was different but captivating. Synthesizers weren't just instruments but alchemists, turning introductory notes into ethereal tones, creating a soundscape as vivid and imaginative as a painter's canvas. Bands like New Order weren't just musicians; they were modern-day wizards weaving spells with every keystroke.

Little did I know, this era of music was not only transforming the airwaves but was a harbinger of the digital age to come. Every synthesized note and every electronically produced melody heralded a future where technology and human creativity would become inseparable. In this world, the boundaries between the organic and artificial weren't just blurred but beautifully intertwined. The synth-pop era was a glimpse into the future, melodically narrating the digital symphony that would shape the world of tomorrow.

Queens of Melody
When Madonna and Whitney Reigned Supreme

The 1980s weren't just a time of musical experimentation and the rise of new genres; they also heralded the crowning of pop royalty. Madonna and Whitney Houston are names that every household would come to know, voices that would serenade us through every high and low of our lives.

I still recall the first time the electrifying beats of Madonna's "Like a Virgin" filled the air. It was at a local diner, and the jukebox was every teenager's musical sanctuary. Though my years of teenage rebellion were behind me, the youthful energy and audacity that Madonna exuded was infectious. The Queen of Pop was as much a visual spectacle as she was a vocal powerhouse. Every music video and every live performance was a marriage of music, fashion, and unabated expression.

Whitney, oh, sweet Whitney! She was a contrast yet a complement to Madonna's theatricality. Whitney Houston's voice was a celestial entity. This unseen force could bring tears to your eyes, inject hope into your soul, and make the heart swell with the euphoria of love. "I Will Always Love You" wasn't just a song; it was an experience, a melodic journey through love's tender, tumultuous, and triumphant chapters.

Now, in the embrace of the years that gift wisdom and retrospection, I marvel at the legacy of these iconic divas. In an era marked by musical innovation and cultural shifts, Madonna and Whitney were more than artists; they were revolutionaries. They didn't just sing songs; they told stories and broke norms, and in every note and every performance, they echoed the sentiments of millions. In their reign, pop music wasn't just entertainment but an anthem of identity, diversity, and the unyielding power of expression. The records may age, but the echoes of their music are immortal, pulsating through time, reverberating the undimmed luminance of the era when the divas of pop reigned supreme.

Echoes of the Underground

The Dawn of Alternative Rock

The 1980s were a loud, colorful, and eclectic time for music. Amidst the glitz of pop and the rebellious riffs of metal, a different sound was quietly brewing, waiting for its moment to echo through the corridors of the music world. That sound was alternative rock, a genre that prided itself on being everything mainstream wasn't.

My introduction to alternative rock came unannounced, an unexpected twist to my well-trodden musical journey. There's a special kind of magic in discovering something that hasn't yet touched the mainstream, like unearthing a treasure waiting to dazzle the world with its uniqueness. Bands like R.E.M. and The Smiths were those hidden gems.

I remember a younger cousin, Brad, a kid with a taste for the eclectic, handing me a mixed tape. "This isn't your usual tune," he'd warned with a wry smile. The cryptic lyrics of R.E.M's "Radio Free Europe" and the sad yet beautiful melodies of The Smiths' "This Charming Man" weren't just songs but reflections of an underlying subculture, a voice giving expression to the quiet unrest and the unsung narratives of the time.

Alternative rock was more than music; it was a sanctuary for those who found solace in the unconventional, the poetic, and the profoundly personal. It wasn't about the dazzling lights or the grand stages; it was about small gigs where the air was thick with the raw, unfiltered passion of artists who sang from the soul, not just the voice.

And as the years unfurled, when the grandeur of the pop stars and the metallic roars of the glam bands have faded into sweet nostalgia, the echoes of alternative rock linger, untainted, unblemished. It reminds us of a time when every chord struck a rebellious note, every lyric was a poetic defiance, and every song was a journey into the soul's deep, often tumultuous waters. In the loud, energetic narrative of the '80s, alternative rock was the quiet, powerful undercurrent that told stories untold and voiced emotions unexpressed. It marked the beginning of a movement as diverse as the era in which it was born.

Harmonies at the Crossroads

The New Chapter of Country Music

The 1980s, oh, what a time! It was a decade where every genre of music was touched by a spell of transformation, even the soulful, grounded notes of country music. The cozy, familiar twang of the guitar and the rustic charm that country songs wafted were now infused with something more universal.

I was a creature of habit, especially when it came to music. I had laid the foundation of my musical taste in the earlier years. In this sanctuary, the melodies of the past lingered. But change, as it always does, knocked on my door with the graceful, powerful voices of artists like Dolly Parton and Kenny Rogers.

I remember an evening painted with the golden hues of the sunset when my wife, Lorraine, beckoned me to listen to a new record. It was Dolly's "9 to 5". Now, I had my reservations; it wasn't the country music I grew up with, but there was something enchantingly irresistible about it. The country roots were unmistakable, yet there was a sprinkle of pop's vivacity.

Kenny Rogers's voice was a bridge between the classic and the contemporary. "Islands in the Stream," a duet with Dolly, was a testament to that. They spun magic, a harmonious blend of traditional country soul with pop's universal appeal. It wasn't just a song but a symphony where the old and the new danced unbridled, unreserved.

This evolution wasn't just audible in the tunes but visible in the arenas. Country stars now filled larger venues, drawing crowds that swayed to the harmonious blend of the old and new. With its new attire, country music was stepping out from the rural landscapes and quaint taverns, gracing the grandeur of universal stages.

These memories linger, echoing the harmonious transition of an era where country music stood at the crossroads. It looked back at its roots, firm and unswayed, and forward to the horizons where new melodies, rhythms, and harmonies awaited. A beautiful reminder that change, though often resisted, is the silent composer of life's most enchanting symphonies.

Echoes of Evolution

The Digital Dawn in Music

As the 1980s unfolded, something extraordinary was stirring in the music world, something that would re-orchestrate the familiar cadences of musical notes into a symphony of new-age sounds. It wasn't just the artists and genres that were riding the waves of change; my dear friend, technology was becoming the unseen conductor, weaving magic into the soul of music.

I remember the evening vividly, the sun bidding farewell with a cascade of golden hues, when my nephew Ben, an enthusiastic young lad with an insatiable appetite for music, bounded into my house, his eyes sparkling with the excitement of discovery. In his hands, he held something that looked unfamiliar yet intriguing - a compact disc, a shiny, sleek testament to the future of music.

That evening, the nostalgic crackle of the vinyl was replaced by the crisp, flawless notes emanating from compact discs. Ben's ecstatic chatter about the clarity, the convenience, and the newfound portability of music painted a vivid picture of an era where technology and artistry would dance to the same tune.

And it wasn't just the format that was transforming. Oh, no. The very creation of music, the soulful strumming of guitars, the haunting echoes of the piano, and the robust beats of the drums were all being touched by the wand of technological innovation. Digital synthesizers and drum machines added new dimensions, breathing an electronic soul into the organic body of musical notes.

There was a sparkle in Ben's eyes as he explained the marvels of this new world, in which the harmonious union of technology and talent would spawn an era of musical wonders characterized by unprecedented precision, diversity, and accessibility.

As I watched the young lad's face, animated with the excitement of a new dawn in music, a wave of nostalgia washed over me. The rustic charm of vinyl records, the tactile pleasure of flipping them over, the intimate imperfections in their notes - were they destined to become echoes of a cherished past?

Yet, amidst the symphony of emotions, a realization dawned - every note of the past, every echo of the present, and every symphony of the future is but a chapter in the enduring saga of music. It is a saga scripted not just by the hands that strum the chords but also by the invisible hands of time and technology that weave new melodies into the timeless soul of music.

PERSONAL MEMORY PROMPT ON MUSIC

A Journey through Melodies

As we meander through the illustrious eras of music, each paragraph infused with the echoes of iconic tunes and legendary artists, there exists an invisible thread weaving through these words, a line connecting each note to a precious memory, each lyric to an unforgettable moment. Yet, every reader, including you, has a unique symphony of memories, a treasure trove of moments painted with distinctive hues, evoking varied emotions.

This section invites you to dive deep into your ocean of musical recollections. These prompts are not just questions; consider them as keys crafted with affection, ready to unlock the chambers of memories where melodies, emotions, and moments lie in serene slumber.

My sincerest desire is to transcend the printed words and resonate with the chords of your heart.

So, I invite you to pause, reflect, and allow these prompts to escort you down the memory lanes. Let's revive, together, the golden eras of music and dance once more amid the echoes of the melodies that defined our yesterdays and continue to enrich our days.

1950s: The Dawn of Rock 'n' Roll and Melodic Harmony

The First Strains of Elvis:

Can you recall the very first time you heard an Elvis song? What were you doing, and how did that melody make you feel?

Jazz and Blues Nights:

Think back to a smoky jazz club or a blues concert. Who were you with, and how did the music move your soul?

1960s: The Decade of Revolutionary Sounds and Iconic Festivals

Beatlemania Moments:

Where were you when The Beatles invaded the airwaves? Do you have a favorite song or album?

Woodstock Wanderings:

Whether you attended or heard tales, what emotions or stories does the iconic Woodstock Festival evoke for you?

1970s: The Era of Disco Balls and Rock Legends

Dancing to the Disco Beat:

Can you remember the dazzling lights and energetic beats of the disco era? What song always got you on the dance floor?

Rock Concert Chronicles:

Close your eyes. You're at a concert of Led Zeppelin, Pink Floyd, or another rock legend. What song is playing, and how does the crowd react?

1980s: The Advent of Pop Icons and Music Videos

Michael Jackson's Thriller Night:

Where were you when you first saw the "Thriller" music video? How did the King of Pop's dance moves and melody captivate you?

MTV Revolution Revelations:

The birth of music videos changed the scene forever. What was the first music video you watched, and how did it make you feel?

Across the Decades: Uniting Generations Through Music

Mixtape Memories:

Remember crafting the perfect mixtape or receiving one? Which songs were must-haves, and what memories are tied to those tunes?

Concert Connections:

Can you recall the electrifying atmosphere of a live concert? Who did you see, and what unforgettable moments unfolded before your eyes?

50S CINEMA

When Icons Were Born

Childhood Glimpses

"Sunset Boulevard" (1950)

I was but a 7-year-old kid when "Sunset Boulevard" graced the big screen. Of course, at that tender age, Hollywood's complexities and dark allure, as portrayed in the film, were far beyond my grasp. My world was simple, filled with the innocent joys of childhood, yet something about that film lingers in the recesses of my memory.

My older siblings were abuzz with excitement, their animated chatter about the movie filling the cozy confines of our living room. They'd huddle with friends, talking about the iconic Norma Desmond, portrayed by the inimitable Gloria Swanson, and her haunting portrayal of a faded silent movie star desperate to return to the screen.

I was too young to join them at the movies, but their excitement was palpable, and it sparked a sense of wonder in my young heart. Though miles away, Hollywood felt like it had entered our small town, igniting conversations and capturing imaginations.

I didn't watch "Sunset Boulevard" until much later. Still, one scene was often recounted by my siblings and the older kids in the neighborhood - the moment Norma Desmond descends the grand staircase, uttering the immortal lines, "Alright, Mr. DeMille, I'm ready for my close-up."

That scene, though heard second-hand, painted a vivid picture in my young mind, as striking as the black and white frames of the film.

Here's a nugget that not many may know - "Sunset Boulevard" was one of the first films ever to feature a narrative structure where the storyteller was not alive. This technique brought a haunting, otherworldly feel to the narrative. It pushed the boundaries of storytelling, ushering audiences into a world where cinema norms were being reimagined.

"Sunset Boulevard" didn't just entertain; it offered a stark, unfiltered gaze into Hollywood's enchanting yet unforgiving world. It was a world that I, as a 7-year-old, had yet to comprehend, but I could feel the charisma it cast, the ripples it sent through the decades. The film is a testament to a Hollywood veiled in an alluring yet elusive mystique, an echo of an era where stars like Norma Desmond glittered brightly yet vulnerably under the scintillating lights of fame.

Each recollection of the film, each shared story from those older and wiser, was a stepping stone into a world of cinema that was as magical as it was mysterious, a world that would, in the years to come, become a sanctuary of stories, emotions, and unforgettable moments for me. The echoes of "Sunset Boulevard" marked the dawn of my journey into the mesmerizing world of the silver screen.

Innocence and Wonder

"Singin' in the Rain" (1952)

At 9, with my world beautifully uncomplicated and curious, a movie like "Singin' in the Rain" was nothing short of magic. I remember the excitement that buzzed in the air; it wasn't just a film – it was an event, a spectacular display of color, music, and dance that would sweep you off your feet and into a world where rain was a companion to dance, and streets a stage for the grandest performances.

I can still recall the first time my eyes beheld the mesmerizing dance of Gene Kelly, splashing and twirling under the downpour with an elegance that made the rain seem like a cascade of sparkling diamonds. I was transported into the cozy embrace of our living room, with my family clustered around the small yet magical box of our television set. The world of black and white that usually graced our screen was painted with the vibrant hues of joy, romance, and the sheer spectacle of cinema.

"Singin' in the Rain" was more than a musical; it was a celebration. Every note and move was like a burst of sunlight through the clouds, illuminating the mundane and the ordinary with an extraordinary glow. Kelly's iconic dance sequence, his feet tapping a jubilant melody on the rain-kissed streets – it was a scene that would dance gracefully into cinematic history.

Here's something you might find delightful – did you know milk was mixed with water to make the raindrops more visible on camera during the iconic rain-dancing sequence? These little behind-the-scenes wonders make the world of cinema so magically intricate.

I was but a child, yet "Singin' in the Rain" infused an affection for the rhythmic embrace of musicals. This genre's stories unfolded through dialogues, melodies, and dances that would echo through time. Each time the sky would adorn the grey attire of rainclouds, and droplets would cascade to the earth, the triumphant notes of Gene Kelly singing the iconic song would play in my head – a melody of joy, an anthem of innocence, and a testament to a time when cinema was a doorway to a world of uncontainable wonder.

In the rainy afternoons that followed, armed with the infectious spirit of Gene Kelly, I too would find myself dancing in the rain, a 9-year-old with dreams as boundless as the raindrops that kissed the earth. "Singin' in the Rain" was not just a film; it was an invitation to find joy, magic, and music in the ordinary, a sentiment that would linger, as enduring as the melody of the iconic song that graced the silver screen that unforgettable year of 1952.

The Real World in "On the Waterfront" (1954)

When I was 11, life was all about playing and imagining. Then, "On the Waterfront" came along. It wasn't like a kid's story. It was real and raw and showed a different, stricter world. I first saw it on a typical Saturday evening, surrounded by my family's chatter. The movie pulled me into a world where good and evil weren't so easy to tell apart.

Marlon Brando was the star. I didn't know who he was back then, but I can't forget the powerful look in his eyes. His character, Terry Malloy, was a man caught up in hard choices and big troubles. "I coulda been a contender," he said. That line, though I was too young to get all of it, made me feel something profound and powerful.

Did you know that this film was more than a story? It was like a quiet protest against McCarthyism, which was trying to control and silence artists back then. This movie told the world that wouldn't be so easy.

"On the Waterfront" didn't have dancing or epic battles. It was a natural, close look at regular folks, their demanding lives, and the choices they made. I didn't understand everything at 11, but the emotions and struggles felt authentic and stuck with me.

As a kid discovering new things, I found this movie to stand out. It wasn't a fairy tale or an adventure story. It was a glimpse into the real world, where life was tough, choices were more complex, and every person had a story worth telling.

Cinema did more than entertain - it opened my eyes, made me feel, and left a lasting mark.

A Peek Into Other Lives with "Rear Window" (1954)

At 11, I thought the whole universe was my small town and the adventures I'd have with friends. Then came "Rear Window," a movie that showed me a different world, one where you could peek into the lives of others right from your window.

I watched it with my big brother, our eyes wide, stuck to the screen. The film was about a man with a broken leg, just watching his neighbors. Sounds simple, right? But oh, it was so much more. He starts to think there's a crime happening right across from him. Can you imagine that? Being stuck, and all you can do is watch?

The man behind this movie, Alfred Hitchcock, was a wizard with a camera. Did you know people called him the 'Master of Suspense'? Every scene, every moment in "Rear Window" was a puzzle piece, and you'd be biting your nails, trying to fit them all together.

The film made my little world grow bigger. It made me curious about people, and I wondered what stories were hiding behind every window I saw. At 11, I was starting to understand - everyone has a tale, and sometimes, they're as thrilling as any detective story.

"Rear Window" wasn't just a movie. For a kid like me, it was a doorway to a bigger, mysterious world full of lives as rich and strange as any storybook tale. And that's the magic of movies. In a dark room, with popcorn in hand, every film is a new world waiting to sweep you away.

Journey to Ancient Times with "Ben-Hur" (1959)

When I was 16, it was all about rock 'n' roll, school dances, and those never-ending dreams of the open road. But one day, everything paused for "Ben-Hur." Suddenly, I wasn't just a teenager in the '50s; I was a prince in ancient times, racing chariots and fighting for honor.

Now, walking into that grand old movie theater, none of us expected the journey we were about to take. The film was over three hours long and was an experience: swords, sandals, epic battles, and a tale of friendship, betrayal, and redemption that felt as grand as the colossal ships and deserts it showcased.

Did you know "Ben-Hur" won 11 Academy Awards? I didn't know much about awards then, but I knew magic when I saw it. The chariot race scene wasn't just on the screen. It was thundering in the theater, every wheel turn, every clash echoing with the raw energy of life and the thrill of cinema.

At 16, you're standing on the edge of tomorrow, but "Ben-Hur" made me look back to a world carved in stone and echoing the tales of heroes. It showed me the grip of the past on the present. This grip turned a rowdy teenager into a wide-eyed witness of cinema's power to transport us across time.

"Ben-Hur" was more than a film; it was a taste of the ancient epics, a hint of the grandeur of the human saga - a saga penned not just in books but in the heartbeat of every scene, every frame of this monumental piece of cinematic art. It was a reminder that within the bustling hallways of high schools and the loud laughter of teenage years, ancient tales were waiting, ready to whisk us away into the epic, the extraordinary.

Silver Screen Legends
The Icons of the 50s

Marilyn's Magic Moment

I was just 10 when I first saw Marilyn Monroe. She was like a burst of sunshine on the monochrome canvases of our post-war days. "Gentlemen Prefer Blondes" was playing at the old cinema down the road. The excitement wasn't just about the movie - it was about Marilyn. With her golden curls, that unmistakable voice, and the sparkle in her eyes that outshone even the brightest stars. Did you know the dress she wore during that iconic "Diamonds Are a Girl's Best Friend" sequence was so tight she had to be sewn into it? Every move, every smile – it wasn't acting. It was magic in motion.

The Rebel, James Dean

Three years later, a new face appeared on the scene - James Dean. I was a teen, full of that quiet storm of rebellion, when "Rebel Without a Cause" hit the screens. Dean wasn't just an actor; he was the voice of every restless soul aching to burst free. I remember his red jacket as vividly as yesterday, a splash of color against the black-and-white world we knew. In that jacket, with those piercing eyes, Dean didn't just act. He told our story.

Audrey's Elegance

And then there was Audrey Hepburn. My goodness, every girl in my school wanted to be her, and every boy, well, we were just smitten. "Roman Holiday" (1953) was the film, and I still remember that charming smile and the elegance that flowed naturally. We were kids, but we felt the magic of Rome and the romance that seemed as eternal as the city itself through Audrey's spellbinding performance. Did you know she did most of her stunts alone, riding that Vespa through the streets of Rome?

Marlon Brando: More Than an Actor

Marlon Brando was an experience. Even as a kid, I could tell there was something special about him. I first saw him in "A Streetcar Named Desire" and boy, was I hooked! His role as Stanley was powerful and raw. It wasn't acting – it felt natural. Brando had a way of getting into the skin of his characters. Watching him was like peeping into the soul of the person he portrayed. It wasn't just about his words but how he made you feel.

Did you know Brando was known for making up some of his lines on the spot? He didn't just stick to the script – he brought something extra, something that made his characters come alive. Every film was a new journey a new person to meet, thanks to Brando's magic touch.

In every role he took, from the tough guy in "On the Waterfront" to the unforgettable 'Vito Corleone' in "The Godfather," he showed us a different side of humanity. And that's what made Marlon Brando a legend. He wasn't just an actor on a screen but a storyteller who made every emotion and moment feel authentic.

In the age of sock hops and soda shops, these icons weren't just stars but companions. They laughed, loved, and rebelled with us, echoing the silent yet tumultuous symphony of the 1950s, where every note was a step into a world reborn from the ashes of war, a world teeming with the raw, untethered spirit of life rediscovered.

60S ON SCREEN

My Journey in the Age of Innovation

A Chilling Encounter

"Psycho" (1960)

At 17, my world was dominated by high school exams, weekend hangouts, and the anticipation of the emancipation that adulthood promised. Amidst this adolescent fervor, I encountered a film that would cast a haunting, unforgettable shadow over my youthful exuberance. The name? "Psycho."

I first saw Alfred Hitchcock's masterpiece with friends at the local cinema. None of us had encountered a film that penetrated the psyche as "Psycho" did. We walked into that theater full of the invincibility of youth. We walked out silent, the chilling notes of Bernard Herrmann's score echoing in the ominous silence.

I remember the unease that the shower scene stirred - a moment imprinted in the annals of cinematic history. It was not just the startling imagery but the eerie silence followed by the piercing, staccato music notes as Marion Crane met her demise. It was art and terror, beauty and horror, masterfully interwoven in a scene that would haunt our dreams and ignite our fascinations.

Did you know Hitchcock used chocolate syrup as blood for that iconic scene? In the black and white film, it had the right consistency and color to give the most authentic effect. "Psycho," a masterpiece of filming, was crafted with a meticulousness that transcended the norm, and each shot was a testament to a director who was sculpting a piece of history.

I was young, on the brink of adulthood. Yet, in those chilling moments, staring at the haunting imagery unfolding before my eyes, I felt the innocence of youth waver. It was a rite of passage, an unsettling yet exhilarating introduction to the raw, unfiltered, mesmerizing world of adult cinema. Hitchcock didn't just entertain; he invaded our thoughts and left an indelible mark that would linger far beyond the closing credits.

Learning Life's Lessons
"To Kill a Mockingbird" (1962)

When I was 19, life felt like a book with pages eagerly waiting to be turned, each chapter promising excitement, challenges, and discoveries. In my own coming-of-age story, I stumbled upon a film that would elegantly mirror the complex dance between innocence and the harsh realities of life - "To Kill a Mockingbird."

I saw it for the first time at a quaint little cinema in the heart of the town. Every seat was filled, the air buzzing with the shared anticipation of movie-goers ready to be whisked away into the world Harper Lee so vividly painted in her iconic novel. The silence was almost palpable as the lights dimmed and the first scene unfolded.

As Atticus Finch, Gregory Peck felt like a father figure, a moral compass navigating the stormy waters of racial prejudice and moral integrity. I was as entranced by his profound wisdom as I was by the youthful innocence of young Scout and Jem. Each scene and each dialogue echoed the deep resonance of life's most complex yet elementary lessons.

Did you know the film's screenwriter, Horton Foote, never visited Monroeville (Harper Lee's hometown and the inspiration for Maycomb)? He wrote the script based on her descriptions and his upbringing in Wharton, Texas. And yet, the portrayal was so authentic that it felt like stepping into the world Lee had immortalized.

At 19, teetering on the edge of adulthood, grappling with my understanding of right and wrong, justice and prejudice, "To Kill a Mockingbird" was an education. Each character and each scenario was a reflective surface, mirroring the complexities of human nature, societal norms, and moral ethics. It was a journey into the depth of human character. This exploration would linger, inspire, and challenge the notions of justice, kindness, and integrity in the years of growth that lay ahead.

Epic Storytelling

Journeys to Distant Lands and Melodic Alps

A Desert Odyssey: "Lawrence of Arabia" (1962)

At 19, the world was a mystery waiting to be unwrapped, and my appetite for adventure was insatiable. That's when "Lawrence of Arabia" made its majestic entry into my life. My buddies and I crammed into the local theatre, popcorn in hand, not knowing we were about to witness something spectacular.

I remember being immediately swept away by the grandeur of the desert, the sweeping sands painting a canvas of mystery and allure. Peter O'Toole didn't just play Lawrence; he became the enigmatic figure, navigating the unyielding desert with a spirit as wild and free as the winds that swept those golden sands.

Did you know the film wasn't shot in sequence? Yet, each scene blended smoothly, like a seamless dance of images and emotions. At 19, my world was expanding, and Lawrence's journey through the dangerous yet beautiful landscapes of the Middle East was a visual metaphor for the adventures and challenges that awaited in the world beyond my doorstep.

Melodies in the Mountains: "The Sound of Music" (1965)

Fast forward to 22, and the tunes of my life found a musical companion in "The Sound of Music." I took my sweetheart, soon to be my wife, to watch this musical masterpiece. The majestic mountains weren't just a backdrop; they were silent characters weaving the tale of the Von Trapp family.

Julie Andrews' voice was a serenade, a melodic journey through life's trials, tribulations, and triumphs. I remember feeling emotion during the iconic "Do-Re-Mi" scene. Did you know Salzburg's residents weren't fond of the filmmakers? Despite this, the film captured the town's beauty in a way that felt like a love letter to the picturesque locale.

Sitting in the dark theater, with the music resonating with the harmonious blend of hope, resilience, and love, the outside world ceased to exist. Every song and every scene was a step into a world where music was an emotion that bridged the gaps between eras, cultures, and histories.

For a young man ready to embark on the journey of marriage, "Sound of Music" was a melodic reassurance of the beauty that resided in the unwritten chapters of life's journey.

A Winter's Tale

"Doctor Zhivago"

At 22, my feet were firmly planted in adulthood. However, my soul was still a wanderer, seeking stories spun with the golden threads of romance and the icy touch of hardship. That's the year "Doctor Zhivago" graced the screen, and oh, what a marvel it was.

I remember it was a chilly evening when my mates and I stepped into the warm glow of the cinema. The air was abuzz with anticipation. From the first scene, we were transported into a world of snow-kissed landscapes and hearts warmed by love, as tumultuous as the revolutions that painted the backdrop of this cinematic masterpiece.

With his piercing gaze, Omar Sharif didn't just portray Zhivago; it felt like he bore the soul of a poet navigating the icy waters of love and war. Did you know the film wasn't shot in Russia but in Spain? The snow was artificial, but you wouldn't guess it!

Every frame of "Doctor Zhivago" was a painting, every note of the soundtrack a pulse that echoed the untamable heartbeats of characters carved from the icy winds of revolution and the warm breezes of romance. At 22, with life's battles and loves ahead of me, "Doctor Zhivago" was not just a film; it was a whisper of the dualities that awaited, where love's warmth and life's cold trials dance in an eternal ballet.

A Cosmic Journey

"2001: A Space Odyssey"

At 25, I was a mix of a young man still eager to explore the stars and an adult anchored by the gravitational pull of responsibilities. That's when "2001: A Space Odyssey" found its way into the cinemas and my life, offering an escape into the stars and beyond.

I still recall the day; my friends and I were curious, always tilting our heads upward, wondering what lay beyond the blue sky. The cinema darkened that evening as we sat with popcorn in our laps. The first notes of the film's iconic soundtrack filled the air. We were no longer in our seats – we were drifting, weightless, in the cosmic dance of the universe.

Kubrick – ah, that man had a wizard's touch! He didn't just direct a film; he sculpted a journey into the stars, where the silence spoke in echoes of wonders untold and terrors unimaginable. The film was a riddle, a poem, a question mark painted against the canvas of the infinite dark.

Did you know Kubrick and Arthur C. Clarke, the story's author, sent a draft of the film's script to NASA? They wanted to get the details right, to weave science and fiction into a tapestry that felt as real as the night sky that greeted us when we stepped out of the cinema, our minds abuzz with questions and wonders.

"2001: A Space Odyssey", for the 25-year-old me, was an invitation to look beyond the known, to imagine the unimagined, and to step into a future where the stars weren't just fiery spheres in the night sky but destinations, each holding secrets, wonders, and terrors waiting to be unraveled.

Stars that Shone Bright

Icons of the 60s

When I think of the 60s, it's as if a glittering constellation of stars appears before my eyes, each shining with its unique brilliance. Elizabeth Taylor, oh, how she shone! I remember being 19 and utterly spellbound by her performance in "Cleopatra" (1963). Her eyes weren't just violet; they were the deep oceans and the infinite skies, a mystery none could unravel. Did you know that the film, as grand as her eyes, almost bankrupted 20th Century Fox? Yet, it became a classic, just like Elizabeth, timeless and unforgettable.

At the same age, another icon stepped into the spotlight, Sean Connery, with the suave and unflappable James Bond in "Dr. No" (1962). Ah, to be 19 and to step into a world of spies, exotic locales, and unmatched charisma. Each scene was a ticket to a world where danger met elegance, and every line Connery delivered was as smooth as the finest whiskey. Did you know Connery wore a wig throughout the Bond films? Yet, nothing could cover his aura of invincibility and charm.

Julie Andrews is a name that rang in our ears with the sweetest melodies. I was 22 when "The Sound of Music" graced the cinemas. Julie was not just an actress; she was a symphony, each note, each scene – a timeless dance of grace and talent. Who could forget those green hills, alive with the sound of music? Fun fact: the last note in the iconic song "Do-Re-Mi" was sung spontaneously by Andrews, a melody unplanned yet unforgettable. The 60s weren't just years; they were painted, each stroke a star, each echoes a memory of icons that weren't just seen but felt, deep in the soul, resonating through ages, the skies, and beyond.

70S FILM

Unleashing New Waves

A Shift in Power

The Godfather (1972)

The 70s marked the start of adulthood, a phase filled with new responsibilities and the inception of my own family. But amidst the hustle and bustle of life, cinema remained a sanctuary. The release of "The Godfather" in 1972, when I was 29, is engraved in my memory, a milestone not just in my life but in the world of film.

I remember sitting in the theater, the air thick with anticipation. As the haunting melody of Nino Rota's score filled the room, an unforgettable narrative of power, family, and crime unfolded. The Corleone family, portrayed with such raw intensity, felt almost natural. Each scene, meticulously crafted, told a tale of loyalty, betrayal, and pursuing the American dream.

The iconic moment when the severed head of a horse appeared in the bed of movie mogul Jack Woltz is etched in my memory. It wasn't just a scene but a powerful message, a dramatic blend of luxury and menace. The Godfather wasn't just a film; it explored the dark corridors of power and crime, leaving audiences both mesmerized and introspective.

This film marked a new era of storytelling, where the lines between heroes and villains were blurred, where characters were deeply flawed yet profoundly human. It wasn't just a movie but a piece of art, echoing the complex symphony of the human condition. Every line uttered, and every scene portrayed remains, to this day, a testament to a time when cinema was not just entertainment but an immersive journey into the intricate dance of light and shadow.

A Dance of Eccentricity

The Rocky Horror Picture Show (1975)

In the mid-70s, at the age of 32, life was a steady rhythm of work and family life. But then came a film that jolted the ordinary, a mesmerizing whirlwind of color, music, and unbridled eccentricity - "The Rocky Horror Picture Show."

I remember the buzz of curiosity that surrounded its release. Friends whispered of its boldness departure from the conventional, and, of course, that caught my interest. One evening, in the company of a group of adventurous souls, I found myself in the dim glow of a theatre, not quite knowing what to expect.

It was apparent from the first scene that this was no ordinary film. It was a heady mix of science fiction, horror, and musical. It was like stepping into another world. Dr. Frank N. Furter, portrayed by the enigmatic Tim Curry, was as charming as he was bewildering.

Songs like "Time Warp" seeped into the fabric of pop culture, a tune that would echo through the ages, a dance that would grace a million floors. The film celebrated the outlandish, a nod to the rebels, and an invitation to embrace the wonderfully weird.

For a 32-year-old navigating the structured world of adulthood, "The

Rocky Horror Picture Show" was a reminder that amidst the schedules and the plans, a world existed where norms were defied, and imagination reigned supreme. It was more than a film. It was an experience, an invitation to a dance of freedom, a call to embrace the spectrum of our existence with open arms and dancing feet.

Unfettered Spirits

"One Flew Over the Cuckoo's Nest" (1975)

1975 was a memorable year for many reasons. Still, cinematically, it presented a piece of art that defied norms and echoed the resilient human spirit - "One Flew Over the Cuckoo's Nest." At 32, juggling the complexities of adult life, this film struck a different, more profound chord.

I recall the experience was akin to being drawn into a world that was both unsettling and deeply human. The confines of the mental institution where the narrative unfolded starkly contrasted with the unyielding spirits of its inhabitants. Jack Nicholson's portrayal of R.P. McMurphy, a character as rebellious as he was relatable, became the embodiment of the indomitable human spirit.

It wasn't a movie you merely watched; you lived it and felt every triumph, every setback, and every rebellion. The stark walls of the institution and the looming presence of Nurse Ratched symbolized those invisible boundaries and judgments we all encountered in real life.

While building a career and family and finding my footing in the world, the narrative reminded me of the innate human desire for freedom, authenticity, and unscripted life. Every laughter and defiance within history resonated deeply, echoing everyday life's silent rebellions and triumphs.

In that darkened theater, amidst the silent rustlings of the audience, a realization dawned - the boundaries, the norms, the expectations - they were as oppressive or liberating as we allowed them to be. In portraying those complex, beautifully flawed characters, a reminder lingered - amidst life's intricacies and expectations, the spirit remained unfettered, untamed, and unyieldingly vibrant.

A New Dawn in Cinema

The Rise of Spielberg and Lucas

Jaws (1975): A Deep Dive into Fear

At 32, I was well into adulthood, enveloped in the rhythm of family and career, yet something stirring and terrifying pulled me back into the spine-tingling thrills of childhood fears. "Jaws" wasn't just a movie; it was an experience that resonated in the depths of our psyches, reminding us of the lurking, unknown horrors of the deep.

As the ominous theme music played, each note echoing the impending doom, I, among millions, was rendered helpless, held captive in the visceral grip of terror. Once a playground of waves and serenity, the expansive ocean transformed into a canvas of lurking dread. Spielberg didn't just direct a film; he orchestrated an experience that would echo in every splash and wave for years.

The simplicity of the storyline was its brilliance: a small town, a lurking predator, and the imminent dance between fear and heroism. At 32, in the calculated predictability of adult life, "Jaws" rekindled the primal, unyielding potency of fear and the exhilarating thrill of facing it head-on.

Star Wars (1977): A Journey to the Stars

Two years later, at 34, another cinematic masterpiece transcended the screen, not to invoke the primal horrors of the earth but to lift the spirits to the infinite realms of space. "Star Wars" wasn't just viewed; it was lived, an epic saga that unfolded not just in the expansive theatres but in the limitless imaginations of millions.

In the silent darkness of space, amongst the clattering of lightsabers and the ominous hum of starships, a galaxy far, far away wasn't a creation of fiction but a tangible, touchable reality. George Lucas had accomplished what few had dared to dream – he made the stars reachable, the galaxies a backdrop of an epic narrative of good and evil.

As I sat there, 34 years of life etched into my existence, the child within was reawakened, the boundaries of reality and fantasy, Earth and space, blurred. Each character became a personal acquaintances, from the wise Yoda to the enigmatic Darth Vader. Their struggles and triumphs were a shared experience.

In the silent aftermath of the rolling credits, the realization was palpable - cinema had changed, and with it, the intricate dance between reality and fantasy. We weren't just spectators; we were participants, catapulted into a universe where the stars were within reach and the galaxies, a playground of untold stories.

Into the Heart of Darkness

"Apocalypse Now" (1979)

At 36, life had its predictable rhythms. Though varied, the roles were well-defined, and the paths were mapped with the clarity of adulthood.

Then came "Apocalypse Now," a journey not just through the harrowing landscapes of war but into the unfathomable recesses of the soul.

I remember the deafening silence of the theater, punctuated by the ominous beating of helicopter blades and the eerie echo of distant gunfire. Coppola didn't just direct a film; he carved a narrative into the collective psyche, forcing us to confront the physical barbarities of war and the haunting specters of our inner demons.

As Martin Sheen ventured deeper into the jungles of Vietnam, we, the audience, were unwilling companions into a descent into madness. Each scene, meticulously crafted, was a mirror reflecting the distorted, horrifying, yet eerily familiar reflections of our hidden selves.

At 36, I was confronted with the unsettling reality: beneath the assured strides of adulthood lurked the tumultuous waters of suppressed fears, traumas, and the unyielding echo of the primal, savage self. "Apocalypse Now" wasn't a film; it was a revelation, a disturbing journey into the depths of the human soul, where civilization was a fragile veneer.

In the disquieting silence post the film's devastating climax, amid the haunting echo of "The End" by The Doors, the realization was inescapable – we were, each one of us, both the hunter and the hunted, the civilized and the savage, the heart of light, and the heart of darkness. In the consuming silence, the boundaries blurred, and I, at 36, was left to confront the unsettling, haunting reflection of my inner apocalypse.

The film did not offer the solace of closure, the comforting delineation between good and evil. As I stepped out into the starry night, the eerie calm was a silent testament to the film's haunting legacy - a journey into the soul's abyss, where answers were elusive. Questions, like the ominous echo of distant drums, were hauntingly persistent.

Stargazing
The Icons of the 70s

Al Pacino's Ascension

The first time I saw Al Pacino, it was as if a lightning bolt had struck the big screen. His role as Michael Corleone in "The Godfather" (1972) was unforgettable, a masterpiece of the changing tides of a character's soul. I was 29, and seeing someone transform before my eyes was captivating. Did you know Pacino was almost not cast in that role? The studios wanted a well-established star, but director Francis Ford Coppola fought for Pacino. And aren't we glad he did?

Jack's Grin

Jack Nicholson - oh, that devilish grin! It was in 1975, I was 32, and "One Flew Over the Cuckoo's Nest" was the talk of the town. Jack's portrayal of Randle McMurphy, a character as wild and untamable as the sea, was electric. Every scene was a dance of rebellion and freedom. Off-screen, Nicholson was just as intriguing. Did you know he discovered that the woman he thought was his sister was his mother?

Diane's Grace

Diane Keaton's effortless grace in "Annie Hall" (1977) caught my eye. I was 34, juggling the roles of adulthood, and there she was – a breath of fresh air. Diane made it okay to be quirky and stylish. Who could forget those iconic outfits and her radiant energy that filled the cinema? Her talent was raw and natural; it felt like she wasn't just acting – she was Annie. A bit of trivia - her real last name is "Hall" and her nickname "Annie." Woody Allen wrote the character with her in mind.

Every era has its stars, but the 70s were a galaxy of talent, each shining with its unique light, shaping a decade of cinematic wonder. Every film was an invitation to step into another world, and oh, the places we went with Al, Jack, and Diane leading the way.

CINEMATIC 80S

My Stories of Revolution

The Birth of Blockbusters
A Journey Through Iconic Adventures

Raiding the Lost Arcs of Cinema (1981)

When "Raiders of the Lost Ark" graced the big screen in 1981, I was 38 – old enough to appreciate the fine art of filmmaking and young enough to get swept away in the adventure. The fedora, the whip, the iconic soundtrack – Indiana Jones was not just a character but a cinematic experience. Harrison Ford brought the adventurous archaeologist to life in ways that lingered, creating a legacy etched in the annals of film history.

Who can forget the boulder chase, a scene that left audiences, myself included, on the edge of their seats, hearts racing in thrilling suspense?

A Friend from the Stars (1982)

The following year, at 39, another iconic character landed on Earth and in the hearts of millions. "E.T. the Extra-Terrestrial" was an emotion. Steven Spielberg had this magical way of weaving fantasy with reality. Who didn't feel that mix of awe and affection when E.T.'s finger touched Elliott's, igniting a glow signifying a friendship that transcended words, species, and planets? That Halloween scene, with E.T. waddling in a ghost costume – it was moments like these that captured innocence, friendship, and the silent echoes of a connection unbroken by the vastness of the universe.

Back to A Future (1985)

When "Back to the Future" rolled around, I was 42. With kids of my own, the cinema became more than storytelling – it was a family experience. Marty McFly and Doc Brown weren't just characters; they were companions on a journey that defied time. Hoverboards, DeLoreans, and the eclectic mix of the past and future – every element was a stroke of genius that painted a world where anything was possible. The clock tower, struck by lightning at the precise moment, became a timeless moment that signified the magic of possibilities, where every second held the power to change everything forever.

Each of these films was a unique gem-adorned the golden era of the 80s, marking the dawn of blockbusters destined to become timeless classics cherished through generations.

Machines and Men

"The Terminator" (1984)

At 41, I remember looking at technology with awe and suspicion. It was a time of rapid advancements, and the line between fiction and reality seemed to blur. "The Terminator," directed by the visionary James Cameron, hit the theaters, making us confront our complex relationship with technology in a visceral, unforgettable manner.

I still remember the dark, intense atmosphere of the movie theater and the hush of anticipation. With his daunting presence, Arnold Schwarzenegger brought the ruthless, calculating cyborg to life, making us question every machine's intent around us. Every beep of the computer and every flicker of the lights felt ominously prophetic. It was science fiction, yet uncannily plausible.

The movie was a heart-pounding journey, a cat-and-mouse chase between man and machine set against the gritty, neon-lit backdrop of 1980s Los Angeles. Every explosion was felt deep in our bones, a testament to the film's pulse-pounding soundtrack and cutting-edge special effects, which were groundbreaking for their time.

The Terminator wasn't just an action movie but a cautionary tale of resilience and the indomitable human spirit. Amidst the staccato of gunfire and the relentless pursuit, there was a subtle yet poignant reminder of our humanity, vulnerability, and unyielding resolve to survive and thrive.

The film left an indelible mark, not just as a cinematic masterpiece but as a cultural touchstone. It made us look at the rapidly evolving world of technology with wonder, anxiety, and a renewed conviction in the human spirit's resilience. With its iconic lines and unforgettable characters, the Terminator became ingrained in the collective psyche, a chilling, thrilling reminder of the dance between man and machine.

A Paranormal Romp
"Ghostbusters" (1984)

When I was 41, something strange and delightful occurred in the cinema. "Ghostbusters" burst onto the screen, filling movie theaters with laughter, wonder, and spooky charm. I can still recall the collective chuckle of the audience, the shared moments of awe, and the iconic, catchy theme song that had everyone humming along.

In a fast-becoming, complicated, serious world, "Ghostbusters" was fresh air. It was a reminder that the mysterious and the unknown could be scary and wildly entertaining. I remember watching Bill Murray, Dan Aykroyd, Harold Ramis, and Ernie Hudson don those iconic jumpsuits armed with proton packs, ready to face the city's spookiest specters with a wink and a smile.

The movie blended the supernatural and the comically absurd, a concoction that shouldn't work but did – spectacularly so. Each ghost, each eerie occurrence, was met with a mix of scientific curiosity and hilarious one-liners. The spooky was made silly, and every creepy entity was as funny as it was fearsome.

I recall leaving the theater with a smile plastered on my face, the iconic logo of the ghost trapped in the red circle and slash imprinted in my memory. "Ghostbusters" was more than just a film; it was a shared experience of laughter, a reminder that even the most otherworldly things could be met with humor and camaraderie. In a decade marked by change and complexity, "Ghostbusters" was a beacon of light-hearted fun, and to this day, I can't help but smile at the iconic line, "Who are you gonna call?"

Teen Angst and Timeless Tales

The Breakfast Club (1985)

In 1985, the world met a brain, an athlete, a basket case, a princess, and a criminal. I was 42, witnessing my teen years being reflected at me from the silver screen, only this time through my children's eyes. John Hughes had this knack, this uncanny ability to peel back the layers of adolescence and expose the raw, tender humanity that lurked beneath the surface.

"The Breakfast Club" was a snapshot of an era. This magnifying glass showed the intricate dance of teenage angst and the tumultuous journey of self-discovery. Every slammed locker, a scribbled note and defiant gaze was a silent anthem that screamed the universal struggles of identity, acceptance, and the desperate search for belonging.

I remember the laughter and the tears that danced in the cinema's darkened hallways. The iconic dance scene in the library, where five disparate souls converged into one unified rhythm, echoed the silent, unspoken solidarity that defies age and time. It was a celebration of misfits and rebels, an ode to every soul that trudged through adolescence's turbulent waters.

Each character was a puzzle piece, an enigma that, when converged, painted a masterpiece of emotion, defiance, vulnerability, and triumph. In those silent moments of reflection, as Simple Minds' "Don't You

(Forget About Me)" echoed, we were all members of The Breakfast Club – bound by an unspoken pact that defied labels, transcending the confines of time to reflect the eternal, unyielding pulse of youth.

An Unlikely Hero
"Die Hard" (1988)

When I turned 45, the film world introduced me and the rest of the audience to an action film that would set the benchmark for many more. "Die Hard," with the charismatic and indomitable Bruce Willis playing the now iconic role of John McClane, wasn't just a movie; it was an adrenaline-charged experience that had us on the edge of our seats from start to finish.

I still remember the thrill, the palpable tension in the air as McClane, barefoot and ordinary yet extraordinarily resilient, battled against all odds in a towering skyscraper. This wasn't your typical hero; McClane was rough around the edges, relatable, and real, and all of us spectators were there with him, feeling every blow and every triumph.

"Die Hard" brought something different. It wasn't just the heart-stopping action sequences or the formidable villain played by Alan Rickman. It was the humanity infused in all that action. I laughed at McClane's witty one-liners, felt the pang of his every injury, and cheered for his every little victory.

In a time where action heroes were often larger-than-life, John McClane stood out as the everyday man. This reluctant hero rose to the occasion, marked by his resilience and wit. To this day, the echoes of "Yippee-Ki-Yay" bring a nostalgic grin, reminding me of that thrilling ride of a film that showed us that heroes come in all forms. Every Christmas, revisiting the chaotic yet heroic journey amidst the decorated halls of Nakatomi Plaza is like a trip back to a time when cinema, in all its explosive action, also made room for a hero who was as real as he was extraordinary.

Riding the Wave of 80s Stardom

With the 1980s came a galaxy of stars who would light up the silver screen with performances that are still cherished today. At the forefront was Harrison Ford. Beyond his iconic role as Indiana Jones, Ford's nuanced performances and dashing charisma cemented him as a Hollywood legend. Who could forget the rush of excitement when he took to the skies in "Blade Runner" (1982), blending the vigor of a hero with the depth of a seasoned actor?

Then there was the rose of the 80s, Molly Ringwald. She wasn't just an actor; to many of us, she epitomizes teenage angst and jubilation. Each role and scene echoed the silent reveries of a generation finding its voice. Molly had this uncanny ability to bring real adolescent emotions to the silver screen, making movies like "Sixteen Candles" (1984) more than just films—they were reflections of our lives.

And in a world where action and fantasy reigned supreme, Arnold Schwarzenegger was king. His portrayal of the ruthless yet intriguing Terminator was iconic, but Arnold was more than just a machine. The audience got a taste of his versatility in "Twins" (1988), showcasing a comedic prowess that left the world both surprised and delighted.

Among these icons, the enigmatic presence of Sigourney Weaver shouldn't go unnoticed. Her role in "Aliens" (1986) proved that heroines could be as fierce and awe-inspiring as any leading man, breaking molds and setting the stage for future generations of female action stars.

In the dynamic panorama of the 80s cinema, these actors weren't just faces on a screen. They were companions in our most intimate moments of joy, sorrow, and discovery. Every line they delivered and every character they brought to life were stitched into the fabric of our memories, forever echoing in the corridors of time.

PERSONAL MEMORY PROMPT ON CINEMA

A Cinematic Journey Together

As we ventured into the cherished terrains of cinematic history, it wasn't just about retracing the steps of iconic films and legendary stars—it became a collective dance of intimate reflections. Every movie, scene, and actor we've revisited is wrapped in layers of emotions and memories, a specific moment that connects us all to the enchanting world of cinema.

These prompts are designed to usher you into a world where the boundaries between the reel and the real blur and the emotions of yesteryears beckon with unyielding allure.

1. The Golden Glimmers of the 50s:

Do you remember first seeing "Sunset Boulevard" or "Singin' in the Rain"? Who were you with, and how did the iconic scenes make you feel?

2. Marilyn Monroe's Magic:

Recall the moment you first saw Marilyn grace the screen. How did her charm and talent capture your imagination?

3. Psycho's Shiver:

Can you recall the spine-tingling sensations during the iconic shower scene in "Psycho"? How did Hitchcock's masterpiece change your perception of thrillers?

4. Musical Melodies of the 60s:

"The Sound of Music" and "West Side Story" marked the decade. Can you remember singing along to the unforgettable tunes? What memories are tied to these musical wonders?

5. A Galactic Odyssey:

When "Star Wars" swept the world, how did it make you feel to witness a galaxy far away for the first time? Did you imagine yourself alongside Luke and Leia?

6. The Godfather's Grip:

What emotions swirled within you during the intense, dramatic moments of "The Godfather"? Did it leave you in awe of the underworld's dark yet enticing realm?

7. Adventures with Indiana Jones:

Do you recall the thrill of venturing into the dangerous yet exciting world with Indy? Which "Raiders of the Lost Ark" scene was etched into your memory?

8. The Teenage Tumult:

"The Breakfast Club" was more than a film; it was a rite of passage. What was happening in your life when you first met the five iconic characters, and how did it resonate with your teenage self?

9. Cybernetic Sensations:

Remember the chilling voice of Arnold Schwarzenegger saying, "I'll be back"? How did "The Terminator" shape your view of the future and artificial intelligence?

10. Ghostbusters' Glee:

Who were you going to call when you first watched "Ghostbusters"? Did the blend of comedy and supernatural ignite a new love for ghostly adventures?

THE MAGIC BOX OF THE 50S

My Window to Wonders

In my early years, the television was a source of magic, unfolding captivating stories right before our eyes. Iconic sitcoms like "I Love Lucy" were not mere shows but portals to a world where humor and charm infused daily life, making viewers laugh heartily together. The '50s marked the dawn of live broadcasts, a novel experience that brought real-time events, though often in fuzzy black and white, into our living spaces, dissolving distances. This era fostered a communal experience where people huddled in anticipation, sharing in laughter and awe. Every episode was more than entertainment; it was a shared memory, an integral stitch in the fabric of our communal experience. In addition to sitcoms and live broadcasts, the 1950s also marked the advent of various notable trends and significant moments in the television industry:

1. A New Era of Information:

I remember my family and I gathered around our small television set to watch "See It Now" with Edward R. Murrow. It was an experience that felt revolutionary - the world's events unfolding before our eyes, delivering news in an intimate and groundbreaking manner. The immediacy and authenticity of television news turned our living room into a window to the world.

2. Childhood Memories:

Oh, the joy and excitement that shows like "Captain Kangaroo" and "The Mickey Mouse Club" brought to my young heart! Every episode was a new adventure, an educational journey veiled in entertainment. These iconic children's programs marked the mornings and afternoons of my childhood, instilling lessons and laughter that echo in my memory.

3. Game Shows Galore:

The thrill of game shows! "What's My Line?" and "The Price Is Right" were not just shows but events that turned ordinary evenings into gatherings of anticipation and excitement. I recall the buzz of engagement, the shouts of guesses, and the shared victories and defeats that made each episode a communal experience.

4. The Family Gathered:

As television sets became more accessible, they transformed our living room into a hub of family bonding. Those memories of us huddled together, our eyes wide with anticipation, are as vivid as the shows we watched. Each program was more than just an episode; it was a cherished moment where time stood still and family bonds strengthened.

5. A Melting Pot of Talent:

I still hear the iconic tunes and laughter from "The Ed Sullivan Show." It was a variety show that was as diverse as it was entertaining. Every Sunday evening, we were introduced to a world of talent, from comedians to musicians, each performance a topic of discussion that would last the entire week. It wasn't just a show but a shared experience that bridged generations and tastes, bringing families and communities together.

Every flicker of the television screen in those days wasn't just about the shows or the stars; it was about the moments we shared, the conversations sparked, and the unified experience of a world discovering the wonders of television together. Those were the days of simplicity yet profound connection, an era where every broadcast was not just entertainment but a stitching together of communal memories.

THE COLORFUL 60S

My Bold New Worlds

I can still remember the awe and amazement of seeing color television for the first time in the 1960s. I was a young adult, and the world seemed to blossom in new and exciting ways. Television was not exempt from this wave of innovation. The vivid hues that once were reserved for cinema screens or our imagination were now splashed across our TV sets, making every broadcast a mesmerizing dance of colors. I was around 17, and this transition felt like stepping into a future where technology and artistry merged to paint our everyday lives with extraordinary shades.

"Star Trek" holds a special place in my memory. The iconic series wasn't just a show but a journey into uncharted territories of space and human potential. Each episode explored the unknown, reflecting the era's quest for discovery and understanding. I recall spirited discussions with friends about space, the final frontier, each of us weaving dreams tinted with the optimism and ambition of youth.

The 60s weren't just about advancements and entertainment; it was a period when television began to mirror the world's complexities. News broadcasts covering the Civil Rights Movement, the Vietnam War, and the moon landing turned our living rooms into spaces of learning, reflection, and sometimes, heated debates. TV was no longer a mere entertainer; it had become a chronicler of our times, capturing the highs and lows, the triumphs and trials with unflinching honesty.

I remember that shows like "The Twilight Zone" provided eerie and fantastical entertainment and piercing social commentary, encapsulating the tumultuous yet hopeful essence of the decade. Television was evolving, and with it, our perceptions of the world, society, and even the galaxies that lay beyond our reach. The transition from black and white to color was emblematic of a world stepping from the shadows of the past into a future teeming with possibilities, challenges, and the unyielding promise of progress. Every new broadcast stepped into a world where reality was as captivating as fiction, and the lines between them were beautifully and profoundly blurred.

RAW 70S

My Era of Emotions and Laughter

In the 1970s, television became an intimate companion, echoing the diversity and intensity of the world around us. It was a decade marked by significant societal shifts, and TV dramas like "MASH" and "All in the Family" weren't just shows; they were reflections of our collective consciousness. Watching "MASH," I remember feeling a mix of emotions - the laughter, the sorrow, and the biting reality of war all encapsulated in a single show. It wasn't just entertainment but a journey into the complex terrains of human emotions and experiences.

"All in the Family" was also a regular watch and a mirror held up to society. Archie Bunker became a household name with his flawed, human, and painfully real character. I remember lively debates around the dinner table, where each episode sparked discussions about social issues, bringing the larger world right into our living rooms.

And ah, who could forget "The Carol Burnett Show"? Every skit was a ticket to a world where laughter reigned supreme. Carol's comedic genius turned ordinary evenings into extraordinary memories, marked by the joyous echoes of laughter. I recall those weekend nights when the whole family, spanning three generations, huddled around the television, basking in the glow of humor that transcended age and time.

The '70s also saw the blossoming of "Saturday Night Live," a show that turned our Saturday nights into a carnival of comedy and satire. I remember the first episode as if it were yesterday, the excitement of witnessing the birth of something revolutionary in television.

The transformation of TV in the 1970s wasn't just about evolving content; it was about television becoming a canvas where the myriad hues of human experience, societal changes, and cultural revolutions were painted in bold, unapologetic strokes. TV was no longer a box but a window to the boundless universe of human stories.

GLAMOROUS 80S

My Youthful TV Adventures

As I ventured into my 40s in the 1980s, television mirrored the extravagance and luxury of the decade. Primetime soaps like "Dallas" and "Dynasty" were grand spectacles that turned ordinary evenings into glamorous affairs. The larger-than-life characters, the intricate plots, and the sheer grandiosity were mesmerizing. I remember settling into the plush comfort of my living room. The lights dimmed as the world of the wealthy and powerful Ewings and Carringtons unfolded before my eyes. Each episode was a delightful escape, an intoxicating mix of affluence, power, and intrigue.

Yet, the '80s weren't just about the glittering world of primetime soaps. They ushered in a new wave of children's programming that became a significant part of family life. Launching networks like Nickelodeon marked the golden era of children's TV. I can still recall the sounds of laughter filling the house as my kids sat, wide-eyed and mesmerized, in front of shows like "Rugrats" and "SpongeBob SquarePants." These weren't just cartoons; they were magical worlds that we, as a family, explored together, stepping into imaginative realms where adventure, friendship, and life's invaluable lessons unfolded in colorful animations.

With its revolutionary concept of music television, MTV turned passive viewing into an interactive experience. I remember watching the iconic "Thriller" music video by Michael Jackson for the first time; it was more than entertainment – it was a cultural phenomenon.

The 1980s buzzed with the glamorous, innocent, wealthy, and adventurous. Television was no longer just a source of entertainment. It had transformed into a multi-dimensional platform where the enchanting dramas of primetime soaps coexisted with the pure, unadulterated joy of children's programming, creating diverse, enriching, and utterly unforgettable memories.

PERSONAL MEMORY PROMPTS ON TELEVISION

Reviving TV Memories Together

We've taken an incredible journey back through TV's golden years together. Now, let's make it even more personal. I've shared my stories and can't wait to hear yours. With "Television Memory Prompts," we'll unlock those special moments that made us laugh, cry, and cheer.

These prompts are friendly nudges to help bring back those cherished memories. Whether it's a favorite episode, character, or theme song, each question is a step back.

We're not just reminiscing; we share a piece of our lives. So, let's dive in, relive those moments, and enjoy this nostalgic journey together!

1. A Classic Comedy Spark

Cast your mind back to the golden age of sitcoms. Can you recall the first time you watched an episode of "I Love Lucy"? What laughter and warmth did those iconic characters bring into your living room?

2. Live and in Color

Remember the marvel of seeing events broadcast live on your TV for the first time? How did that real-time connection to the world expand your horizons?

3. A Technicolor Transition

The '60s introduced us to the colorful spectacle of TV shows in vibrant hues. Can you remember a favorite show that was transformed by color? How did it change your viewing experience?

4. Embarking on the Final Frontier

"Star Trek" not only launched spaceships but also a legion of dedicated fans. Were you one of them? What adventures and characters still linger in your memory?

5. Drama on the Small Screen

The '70s brought complex, emotional TV dramas into our homes. Does a particular episode of "MAS*H" or "All in the Family" still stir your emotions? How did these shows reflect the era's social changes?

6. Variety and Laughter

How often did the skits of The Carol Burnett Show have you doubled over in laughter? Can you remember a sketch or character that still makes you smile?

7. Soapy Evenings

Primetime soaps of the '80s, like "Dallas" and "Dynasty," were larger than life. Who were your favorite characters, and how did their dramatic escapades keep you glued to the screen?

8. Saturday Morning Cartoons

Those Saturday mornings might be sacred if you were a child or had children in the '80s. Can you still hear the theme songs of those iconic cartoons? Which one was your favorite?

9. Nickelodeon Nights

The launch of networks dedicated to children's programming was a game changer. How did shows from Nickelodeon or similar networks influence your family's viewing habits?

10. An Evolving Medium

How did television evolve from a novel invention to a staple of everyday entertainment from the 1950s to the 1980s? Can you pinpoint a moment or show that epitomizes this transformation for you?

Chapter 2

A World Unfolding

In this chapter, we step into the unfolding tapestry of our shared history, revisiting moments that define generations and continue to shape our identity. From global happenings to the intimate narratives of American life, each section unfolds not just my reflections but resonates with the echoes of collective memory.

We journeyed through the echoes of conflict in the '50s, the triumphs and tribulations of the '60s, the dance amidst trust and trials in the '70s, and the illuminating and shadowy narratives of the '80s. Each decade, a story not just lived individually but woven into the fabric of our shared existence.

This isn't a monologue but a dialogue, an intimate space where the historical and personal intertwine. It's an invitation to read, relive, rediscover, and resonate with each event because our stories are intertwined. In these pages, they find a voice and a space to breathe, remember, and be acknowledged.

THE 50S

My Walk Amidst Echoes of Conflict

The Shadows of the Korean War (1950-1953)

I was but a child when the winds of war, chilly and ominous, breezed through the global corridors, making their echoes felt even in my family's cozy, humble abode. The Korean War was a confrontation not as universally chronicled as the World Wars or Vietnam. Yet, its tremors were profoundly felt and weaved into the fabric of everyday American life.

I was too young to grasp the gravity of war fully, yet old enough to sense the somber mood that hung heavily in the air. Our tiny black and white television, a prized family possession, flickered with news updates about far-off battles, echoing with the stern voices of newscasters painting a grim picture of a divided Korea.

My Uncle Richard, a WWII veteran, would sit silently, his eyes reflective, absorbing the broadcasted images of young men, not much older than his sons, marching in a distant land. I didn't understand it all, yet the gravity in Uncle Richard's gaze, the silence that hung in the air post-broadcast, spoke volumes of the unuttered sentiments, the residual echoes of a war he had fought, now mirrored in a new generation.

In the schoolyards, the war infiltrated our innocent plays. Soldier games were infused with a sad undertone, a reality far from the romanticized combat we often emulated. A conspicuous silence, a flag at half-mast, and a community in muted grief followed each news of fallen soldiers. The Korean War might not have been "our war" as kids, yet its specters danced in the silent spaces of our young lives.

Did you know this was the era of "The Forgotten War"? It's a term often associated with the Korean War, encapsulating the conflict's overshadowing by the grand narratives of World War II and the subsequent Vietnam War. Yet, in the silent pauses of Uncle Richard's gaze, the anxieties echoing in the rapid rhythm of mother's knitting needles, this war was far from forgotten. Each echo of the bugle, every clip of soldiers marching in monochromatic footage, bore testament to a conflict that, though distant, was intimately felt in the silent, shadowed corners of American homes."

The Ripples of the Geneva Conference (1954)

As preteen, international conferences and the intricate ballet of diplomacy were far beyond the boundaries of my world, which was filled more with adventures in the backyards and the stories spun by the comic books. Yet, even in that age of innocence, I recall the whispered gravitas accompanying the mentions of the Geneva Conference of 1954. This distant yet persistent echo subtly underscored the adults' conversations around me.

Uncle Richard, who was ever the font of both wisdom and stories in our family, had a certain silence about him whenever Vietnam was mentioned. You see, he knew, perhaps with a soldier's sixth sense, that the decisions made in the plush environs of Geneva would echo in the jungles and rice fields of a divided land.

I was barely eleven, but I remember sitting on the porch, the summer air heavy with humidity and the weight of history being scripted oceans away. Mother would listen to the radio broadcasts, her knitting needles momentarily stilled, each stitch a silent testament to the unspoken anxieties of the Cold War.

Did you know that the partitioning of Vietnam at the 17th parallel was meant to be temporary? It was seen as a brief pause, a fleeting silence before the storm, and not the onset of a war that would capture the global consciousness and define a generation.

I didn't fully grasp the enormity then. Still, in the silent contemplation of Uncle Richard, the terse discussions over the dinner table, and the radio broadcasts painting pictures of divided nations and silent battlefields, I felt the first stirrings of a world expanding beyond the comic books and backyards - a world where history was alive, palpable, and inescapably intertwined with our everyday lives. Each decision, every accord, wasn't just a headline; it was a ripple that would travel across oceans, shaping lives, narratives, and the very era I was growing up in.

A Star in the Cold War Sky - The Launch of Sputnik (1957)

Fourteen years old and with eyes wide as the universe, that's how old I was when 'beep-beep' sounds from a metal sphere orbiting Earth became the world's eerie lullaby. 1957 wasn't just the year of tail fins and rock 'n roll; it was the year humanity, and a teenage me, looked up and realized the stars weren't so far away.

I can still feel the chills, a mix of awe and a tinge of anxiety, as the news of Sputnik's successful launch by the Soviet Union permeated every corner of our small town. We were in the throes of the Cold War, and now, it seemed, the battlefront had extended beyond our Earth into the silent, infinite realms of space.

In the quiet evenings, we'd gather in our backyard, necks craned upwards, half in wonder, half in silent apprehension. Uncle Richard, back from the echoes of Korea and a silent witness to the whispers of Geneva, would join us. His gaze blended the warrior's bravery and the dreamer's awe.

Did you know that Sputnik, though a marvel, was no larger than a beach ball, yet its echoes were planetary? Its beeping signals, piercing through the cosmic silence, were received by radios worldwide, including the old, crackling set in our living room.

It wasn't just a satellite; to my young mind, it was a harbinger of an age where comic book fantasies met stark political realities. Schoolyard's talks shifted from superheroes to stars, space, and the silent 'beeps' that reminded us of a race beyond borders, ideologies, and earthly confines.

Every 'beep' from Sputnik reminded us of a world enlarging before our eyes, where the stars weren't just the stuff of telescopes and imagination but arenas of conquests and contests. The Cold War had a new frontier; for a teenage boy, the universe became both a playground and a battleground of infinite possibilities and silent apprehensions.

A Union Across the Seas

The Formation of the European Economic Community (1957)

My understanding of international politics and economics was still in my infancy as a teenager. Yet, there was something profoundly captivating about the events that unfolded in 1957. We were still amidst the recovery from the war, and the echoes of conflict and camaraderie resonated in the daily lives and stories of our neighbors, family, and friends.

One fine evening, amidst the hum of the radio and the chatter of adults, I first heard of the Treaty of Rome. Still dusting off the debris of devastation, six European nations embarked on an unprecedented journey of unity - they were laying the foundational stones of the European Economic Community.

In our small town, Europe seemed like a world away. Yet, the allure of unity, of nations binding together to weave a tapestry of economic and political solidarity, held a certain magic. I remember Uncle Richard, a man of few words but profound insights, mulling over the newspaper, his brows arched in reflection. “It’s a new world we’re stepping into, kid,” he’d said, the crinkles by his eyes deepening.

There was a subtle but discernible shift in the air. Conversations over dinner tables, dialogues in town meetings, and debates in school corridors bore an undercurrent of change, a silent acknowledgment of a world rapidly transforming. We witnessed the reshaping of nations and redrawing boundaries, not just of territories but of ideologies and alliances.

An interesting tidbit that not many may recall is that the signing of the Treaty was hurried along, done earlier than planned, to avoid the negative press and public opinion influenced by a referendum in France. The urgency and the behind-the-scenes scurries of diplomats and politicians underscored the magnitude and gravity of these six nations’ commitment.

Though young and distant from the epicenter of these monumental changes, the formation of the European Economic Community was one of those historical junctures that hinted at the interwoven destiny of nations. A whisper of a world where borders were not just lines on a map but bridges to new alliances, opportunities, and shared journeys.

MY 60S TALE

Triumph and Tribulations

On the Brink

Living Through the Cuban Missile Crisis (1962)

At the tender age of 19, with the world just beginning to unfold before me, the Cuban Missile Crisis was a jolting reminder of the fragility of peace. It was a moment where the piercing reality of global politics and nuclear threats punctured the cloak of youthful invincibility.

I recall the somber tone of President Kennedy's voice as it echoed from our family's television set, each word heavy with the burden of impending catastrophe. Like millions of others, my family and I were glued to our seats, hanging onto every utterance. The proximity of nuclear arsenals, just a stone's throw away in Cuba, cast an ominous shadow of foreboding that seeped into every American home.

The silent dinner tables, the apprehensive glances exchanged among neighbors, and the haunting specter of mushroom clouds unveiled a story untold by news reports. In those tense days, life seemed to pause; breaths were held, prayers whispered, and hopes clung to the fragile thread of diplomatic negotiations.

A fact not often spotlighted is that U.S. military forces were at DEFCON 2, the second-highest defense readiness condition, where war is just a step away. As a teenager, the technicalities of diplomatic and military jargon were beyond me. Still, the gravity of the situation, the undercurrent of fear, was palpable, even to young souls.

In classrooms, conversations veered from youthful escapades to the chilling prospect of a nuclear confrontation. Teachers' voices, an amalgamation of reassurance and concealed anxiety, led us through drills, instructions underscored by a gravity that rendered the school's corridors eerily silent.

Those thirteen days in October 1962 were a passage from the insouciance of post-war prosperity into an abrupt awakening. With all its technological advancements and diplomatic alliances, the world was still on the edge of destruction. The Cuban Missile Crisis wasn't just a chapter in history books – it was a lived experience, a collective holding of breath, an intimate dance with the unimaginable that left an indelible mark on the soul of a generation.

1963

A Nation Mourns - The Day We Lost JFK

The crisp autumn air of November 22, 1963, carries with it a heavy silence that still lingers, a silence that marked the tragic loss of President John F. Kennedy. I was a young adult, just stepping into the world with wide eyes and higher hopes. President Kennedy was not just a leader but an icon of youthful vigor, hope, and charm. To us, he symbolized a future as bright as his charismatic smile.

I can vividly recall the moment the devastating news broke. The black and white images on the television, blaring in every household, spoke of a national tragedy we could hardly fathom. Our beloved president, JFK, was assassinated in broad daylight in Dallas, Texas. I remember looking at my mother; she had teary eyes and trembling hands clutching the edges of her apron. It was a moment of collective grief, a national heartbreak that pierced every American soul.

Classes were canceled, businesses closed, and the nation was glued to their TV sets, watching the tragedy unfold in real time. Walter Cronkite delivered the shattering news with a trembling voice and moist eyes. I can still recall his voice cracking as he pronounced the president dead - a moment imprinted in the annals of history.

Did you know Kennedy was the youngest man ever elected to the presidency and the youngest to die in office? His untimely demise echoed the end of the youthful exuberance and hope he had instilled in our nation. A somber silence reigned in every corner of the country, from the bustling cities to the quietest rural areas. We were united in our grief, bound by the collective heartbreak, a shared loss that transcended all divides.

As the nation mourned, we watched the young John-John salute his father's casket - a poignant image forever etched in our memories. We were not just witnesses to the assassination of a president; we were a nation mourning the abrupt end of an era of hope, the Camelot years dashed, leaving behind a lingering cloud of 'what could have been.' Every anniversary of that tragic day, as the autumn leaves fall, we are reminded of a young president, frozen in time, who left the world too soon.

A March Towards Equality

Witnessing the Rise of the Civil Rights Movement

The 1960s was a chapter written in bold strokes, where voices clamoring for change resonated through every street, every city, and every heart in America. It was the age of the Civil Rights Movement, a pivotal moment in our history where the quest for racial equality took center stage. Born in the forties, by the time these monumental events unfolded, I was in my twenties, old enough to understand and to be moved by the profound journey unfolding before our eyes.

I remember witnessing the sea of people, thousands upon thousands, assembling in Washington, a human tide of diverse faces but united hearts. They were there to hear a man, not just any man, but Martin Luther King Jr., a voice of peace amidst the turbulent waves of racial injustice. His "I Have a Dream" speech wasn't just heard; it was felt, echoing the collective yearning for a nation where equality wasn't just a word but a lived reality.

In my home, we sat around the radio, the atmosphere thick with anticipation. And then, his voice, clear and resonant, painted a picture of a world where the "sons of former slaves and the sons of former enslavers" could sit together in brotherhood. Even at a young age, the gravity of those words and the dream he articulated felt monumental.

Did you know Martin Luther King Jr. improvised a major part of his iconic speech? Yes, the most memorable segments were delivered spontaneously, a testament to the raw, unscripted passion that defined the movement.

When he spoke of his dream, it wasn't a scripted rhetoric but a heartfelt outpouring that mirrored the silent drives in millions of hearts.

The following year, in 1964, we celebrated another milestone. The Civil Rights Act was signed into law, breaking down legal barriers that had kept African Americans as second-class citizens for centuries. I remember my family, my community, and our collective sense of triumph. The optimism was palpable, a hope that perhaps, we were on the cusp of witnessing the America that Dr. King dreamt of – united, equal, just.

Each event, each speech, each march wasn't just a news headline; they were stitches weaving the fabric of modern America, echoes of a past where division reigned, and the hopeful notes of a future symphony where every citizen, regardless of their color, could play a harmonious part.

On War's Edge

America's Deepening Dance with Vietnam

In the flower of my youth, the specter of war cast long shadows that reached even the quiet suburbs where I lived. The escalation of the Vietnam War was not just a military affair but a social and cultural quake that tremored through the hearts and homes of countless Americans. I was in my twenties, navigating the bridge between youthful idealism and the harsh terrains of adult reality.

The year was 1965, the drums of war rolled louder, and the number of American boots on the Vietnamese soil multiplied. Our boys, neighbors, friends, sons, brothers – they were called to fight a war across the ocean, in lands unfamiliar, for causes debated. Dinner table conversations, once light and filled with the trivialities of everyday life, were now dominated by the nightly news broadcasts painting grim images of the escalating conflict.

I remember the night my friend Johnny, a lad with a smile as wide as the horizon, came over to say he'd been drafted. His voice tremored, not with fear, but a profound uncertainty. The war was no longer a distant event; it had walked through our front doors, sat at our dining tables, and now wore the faces of loved ones.

Did you know that the draft cards, those pieces of paper assigning futures and determining fates, were sometimes burnt in public protests? Yes, in pockets of defiance, young men and their supporters made a fiery declaration of their dissent. These flames, though small, bore witness to a nation divided, a public conscience wrestling with the morality and justification of the war.

As the war raged, another battle unfolded at home. Protests, not just on the streets but in our hearts' silent, questioning spaces. Every broadcasted image of napalm fires, every letter home bearing silent testimonies of distant horrors, begged the question - why? I remember the marches, not with the detachment of a viewer, but as a participant, a young soul amidst a sea of faces, each echoing silent questions, fervent hopes, and impassioned pleas for peace.

Vietnam wasn't just a war; it was a fracture, a painful incision in the heart of America. Yet, amidst this division, in the spaces between the echoing chants of protests and the somber notes of bugles honoring the fallen, America was also finding its voice, loud, unyielding, an anthem of a generation that dared to question, to hope, and to dream of peace.

1969: A Leap Beyond the Stars

The Day We Touched the Moon

In the sweltering summer of 1969, I huddled around our family television set, eyes wide and breath held like millions around the globe. The Apollo 11 mission was not just another space expedition; it embodied humanity's indomitable spirit, our unyielding quest to reach beyond our earthly confines. The moon, that silvery sentinel of the night sky, a muse for poets and a mystery for scientists, was within our grasp.

I recall the grainy images flickering on the screen the palpable anticipation that charged the air we breathed. In those moments, perched on the edge of our seats, we were not just individuals, families, or neighbors - we were united humanity, suspended in the shared breath of anticipation.

Neil Armstrong's voice, crackled yet clear, echoed not just in our living room but in the annals of history. "That's one small step for man, one giant leap for mankind." Those words weren't merely a statement but an epochal testament of human achievement, a collective ascent into the stars.

Did you know that Armstrong and Aldrin spent 21 hours on the lunar surface and brought back 47.5 pounds of lunar material? That night, as those astronauts planted the American flag on the moon's silent surface, it wasn't just a national emblem fluttering in the cosmic winds; it was the flag of every dreamer, every visionary, every silent observer of the starry skies, marking a conquest not of territory, but of potential.

Even decades later, the memory of that giant leap lingers, not just as a testament to American ingenuity and determination but as a reminder of a moment when the eyes of the world turned skywards, collectively marveling at the audacity of the human spirit. We weren't just onlookers; we were, each one of us, participants in a dance with the cosmos, breaching the silent barriers of space to the melodic tunes of human triumph.

70S TAPESTRY

My Dance Amidst Trust and Trials

Trust Betrayed

Inside the Shadows of Watergate (1972-1974)

In the early 70s, the political atmosphere in America was as thick as a foggy morning in San Francisco. I was not that naive young boy anymore; I was in my late 20s, and the winds of political change and turmoil were something I could understand and feel in my bones. The revelation of the Watergate scandal was like a storm that struck with shock and awe. President Nixon, a man elected to the highest office, was accused of unspeakable betrayals.

I remember the buzz of conversations, the heated debates in diners, the intense discussions that infiltrated every gathering. The revelation that the president's men were involved in a break-in at the Democratic National Committee headquarters - was more than a headline; it was a wound.

Uncle Richard, always the political enthusiast in the family, was visibly shaken. The discussions at family dinners were charged, voices raised in anger, and a profound sense of betrayal. Trust, the foundational bedrock of our democracy, felt like it had crumbled. Every revelation and headline was another crack in the facade of integrity we held dear.

One trivia that always sticks with me: Did you know that "Deep Throat," the secret informant who helped journalists Bob Woodward and Carl Bernstein uncover the scandal, remained anonymous for over 30 years? It added an element of mystery to the already dramatic political saga.

When Nixon resigned in 1974, it wasn't a moment of jubilation but reflection. As a nation, we were like a ship in turbulent waters, navigating through the storm, hopeful yet cautious of the dawn that awaited. It was a time of reckoning, a period where America took a long, hard look in the mirror, confronting the imperfections and the vulnerabilities that lay bare before the world and, more importantly, its citizens.

Fueling Uncertainty
The Year Oil Stopped Flowing (1973)

By 1973, I had grown accustomed to the rhythms of adult life. Yet nothing could have prepared me for the oil crisis that suddenly jolted our nation. It was as if the pulsating lifeblood of our bustling America had been choked, leaving an unsettling stillness in its wake. Cars, the symbols of American freedom and progress, sat silent, forming solemn rows at gas stations.

The Organization of Arab Petroleum Exporting Countries had proclaimed an oil embargo, a term that until then, for many of us, was buried deep in the business pages of newspapers. Now, it screamed from every headline and echoed in every conversation. Gas became as precious as gold.

I recall the long lines, the rationing, and the pervasive sense of vulnerability that swept over us.

It's strange how trivial things become monumental in moments of scarcity. My father's old gas-guzzling Chevy became a relic of a bygone era, a symbol of the unbridled opulence we once took for granted. Every drop of gas was accounted for; every trip was calculated for its absolute necessity. Conversations at home and in the community were doused with a new caution, a realization of our dependence on a resource we had so nonchalantly consumed.

Here is a piece of trivia I stumbled upon years later: Did you know the crisis prompted the U.S. to fill the Strategic Petroleum Reserve, an emergency fuel storage of oil to counter future disrupted supplies? It's a realization of how significant the shock of '73 was, a jolt that spurred immediate reactions and long-term strategic shifts.

The embargo didn't just strain our engines; it tested our spirits. But like all adversities, it also uncovered a resilience, a collective will to adapt, and the indomitable American spirit that refused to be dimmed by darkened streets or silent engines. We learned and adjusted, and amidst the chill of the crisis, the seeds of future innovations and evolutions were unwittingly sown.

A Bridge Over Divides

The Helsinki Accords Unfold (1975)

The '70s were years of tumult, marked by the echoes of the Watergate scandal and the pervasive anxiety from the oil crisis. Yet amidst these testing times came a shimmering ray of diplomacy, illuminating the global stage - The Helsinki Accords of 1975. I was now a grown man, balancing the rigors of work and family, yet still attuned to the profound shifts echoing around the world.

The Accords weren't just about high-level diplomacy; they made their presence felt in our living rooms, injecting a subtle optimism into the conversations echoing within the familiar four walls of our homes. In those years, the Cold War wasn't an abstract political terminology; it was a tangible, frosty silence that often hung heavy in the international air.

But here was a pact, a promise that extended beyond territorial boundaries and ideological divides. We watched, perhaps with skepticism and hope, as leaders from the East and West came together, penning commitments to peace, sovereignty, and human rights. It was a sight that bore the promise of a thaw, even amidst the prevailing cynicism.

I remember my family gathered around the television, absorbing scenes of leaders from 35 nations, including the U.S. and Soviet Union, extending hands across the immeasurable ideological chasms. Conversations were charged with a cautious optimism. Could this be the beginning of a new chapter? The Accords weren't binding, but they carried the weight of a shared commitment, an acknowledgment of a shared humanity even amidst the starkest divisions.

Here's a snippet that might intrigue you - the Accords weren't just a political document. They also birthed unprecedented cultural exchanges between the East and West. An aspect less touted but profoundly impactful. It was as if, beneath the political rhetoric, art and culture wove silent threads of connection, expressing a shared human essence that politics often muffled.

Though the tangible impacts of the Helsinki Accords were debated, in those moments of signatures and handshakes, watching from our living rooms, we tasted a morsel of possibility - a world where cold wars could thaw, and bridges could arch over even the most formidable divides. It was a moment where history whispered – in silent yet unyielding echoes – the latent power of unity amidst diversity.

1979: Echoes of Revolution
Witnessing Iran's Profound Transformation

As the '70s drew to a close, the tremors of change resonated from the Middle East, stirring intense dialogues in every corner of the globe, including the quiet simplicity of our homes in America. The Iranian Revolution wasn't just a headline; it was a narrative that unfolded live as international relations, oil politics, and age-old traditions interwoven in a complex dance.

I was well into my thirties then, with the palpable energies of youth giving way to the contemplative reflections of mid-adulthood. The revolution wasn't a distant occurrence; it spiraled through the sinews of our daily lives, influencing conversations at family dinners and fuelling animated discussions in my social circles.

The Shah, a familiar figure in global politics, was now ousted. Images of vehement protests, impassioned cries for change, and Ayatollah Khomeini's stern yet charismatic visage dominated the media landscape. Every update was a fresh, enigmatic chapter of a story weaving through mystery, fear, anticipation, and awe. This wasn't just Iran's revolution but a global spectator's journey through the unpredictable paths of radical transformation.

Little is often recounted about the forces that spurred the revolution. It wasn't just a religious uprising but a chorus of voices from various walks of life. Communists, secularists, and students were all part of this complex mosaic of revolt. Though momentarily unified, this diversity foreshadowed the multifaceted challenges that would mark Iran's journey post-revolution.

And who could forget the hostage crisis that ensued, stamping an indelible mark on U.S.-Iran relations? It wasn't just a political standoff; for us, it was a poignant narrative of human lives trapped in the intricate dance of international diplomacy. Every bulletin and update was a chapter of a lived saga, connecting us, however distantly, to the unfolding narrative in Iran.

In the aftermath, sitting amidst the serenity of my living room, with the chills of the Cold War still resonant, the Iranian Revolution echoed as a potent reminder of a world in perpetual motion. Every nation and every populace was a distinct narrative. Yet, we were all elements in this intricate global patchwork, connected, affected, and invariably intertwined.

The revolution wasn't just Iran's story; it was a chapter in the grand narrative of our interconnected human journey.

THE TURBULENT 80S

My Shadows and Lights

When the Earth Roared

Witnessing the Fury of Mount St. Helens (1980)

I remember it as if it were yesterday. May 18, 1980, was a Sun day for rest and tranquility. Yet, the earth had other plans. The majestic Mount St. Helens, a beautiful slumbering giant nestled in the serene landscapes of Washington State, awoke in a fit of rage that day. I was 37, and never before had I borne witness to Mother Nature's awe-inducing power and furious might.

From where we were, safe in our homes, the eruption was an ominous spectacle unfolding on our television screens, a stark contrast to the usual placidity of our surroundings. Smoke, ash, and fire painted apocalyptic images in the skies, an ethereal dance of destruction that held us captive, suspended between awe and terror.

I recall my children's faces, eyes wide, reflecting the ominous dance of grey and fiery red illuminating the skies, their innocence interrupted by the untamable forces of nature. We were thousands of miles away from the eye of the storm, yet the chilling embrace of the eruption held the nation in a collective gasp.

The aftermath painted a scene of desolation; forests, once lush and teeming with life, now stood silent, their verdant splendor buried beneath a heavy blanket of ash. News reports showed us the devastation; lives, wildlife, and entire ecosystems drastically altered in the blink of an eye.

Did you know that the explosion released energy equivalent to 1,600 times the size of the atomic bomb dropped on Hiroshima? Yet, amid the devastation, there lies a testament to the indomitable human spirit and the relentless pursuit of rebirth. The areas around Mount St. Helens have since transformed into a rich research and education hub, breathing renewed life into a landscape marred by destruction.

In those moments of collective witness, as ash fell like silent rain, we were reminded of the humbling power of nature and the impermanent, fragile essence of our existence - a profound realization that has lingered, haunting and humbling, long after the skies cleared and the earth stilled.

The Day Chernobyl Darkened the Skies (1986)

There are events that, no matter where in the world they occur, hold the collective conscience of humanity in a vice grip of silent disbelief. The Chernobyl Nuclear Disaster was one of those catastrophic instances. I was 43, embedded in family life and career rhythms, when the news of the explosion at the Chernobyl Nuclear Power Plant in Pripyat, Ukraine, spread across the globe like the ominous radioactive cloud that billowed from its epicenter.

Though oceans away, the disaster's echoes permeated the air in America. Every news channel, every radio station, every conversation was veined with a palpable tension, the kind that permeates the atmosphere when the invincibility of human innovation is shattered, laying bare our vulnerabilities.

I remember gathering with the family around our television, watching in stunned silence as the horror unfolded. The grainy images of brave souls heroes who ventured into that silent war of invisible enemies - radiation - displayed a confrontation that felt as profound as the historical wars fought with weapons and might.

Did you know that over 600,000 workers, often called 'liquidators,' risked their lives to contain the contamination and avert an enormous catastrophe? The magnitude of human sacrifice and the silent bravery became stories whispered in hushed tones, echoing the unspeakable impact of the disaster.

On the brink of their journeys into the world, my children watched with faces of confusion and concern. The invulnerable world of their childhood was now tainted with questions, fears, and the stark reality of human fallibility. The Chernobyl disaster was not just a Soviet tragedy but a global awakening, a grim dance of invisible particles that knew no borders no ideologies.

For us, the silent skies of those days bore the invisible specters of radiation. The world suddenly seemed a little smaller, the connections between us all a little stronger, and the need for unity in the face of shared vulnerabilities profoundly urgent. The haunting echoes of Chernobyl linger, a silent reminder of the intersection of human ambition, power, and the unforgiving, impartial laws of nature.

Secrets and Shadows

Navigating the Maze of the Iran-Contra Affair (1985-1987)

At 42, having lived through the Cold War, Watergate, and the societal shifts of the 60s and 70s, I thought I grasped the intricate dance of politics and power. Yet, the revelation of the Iran-Contra Affair was a jolting reminder of the veiled corridors of power that operated far beyond the public's gaze, weaving a complex web of secrets and decisions that would shape our nation and the world.

The details unraveled like a spy novel, each headline revealing another layer of complexity, another twist in a plot that involved the clandestine sale of arms to Iran and the covert funneling of proceeds to Contra rebels in Nicaragua. It was a dance of shadowy alliances and secret dealings that seemed to echo the enigmatic espionage tales of the Cold War era.

I remember the conversations where neighbors and friends, draped in the fabric of their perspectives and beliefs, dissected each revelation, each confession. Did you know senior officials were convicted but later pardoned in President George H.W. Bush's final days? The narrative was as contentious as it was complex.

In the middle of it all, I reflected on the fragile nature of truth, the complex dance of ideology and ethics, and the silent, often invisible threads that weave the narrative of our nation's history. For me, my family, and millions of Americans, the Iran-Contra Affair was not just a political scandal; it was a collective journey through the murky waters of trust, power, and the haunting question of what lurks in the corridors of silent decisions made in the enigmatic halls of power.

Crumbling Divides

The Fall of the Berlin Wall (1989)

As the cold embers of the Cold War began to wane, 1989 emerged as a year of rampant transformation. At 46, with eyes that had beheld decades of tumultuous change, nothing prepared me for the momentous evening when the Berlin Wall, that enduring edifice of division, began to crumble. It wasn't just concrete and barbed wire tumbling; it was an era, a mindset, a world defined by stark lines of ideological battle.

I recall the grainy images on the television screen, the ecstatic faces of Germans, East and West, wielding hammers and picks, each striking a blow against years of imposed separation. Our living room became a sanctuary of silent witnesses as we, a family nestled thousands of miles away, were seamlessly integrated into the fabric of history unfolding in real-time.

Did you know that some parts of the Wall were chipped away as souvenirs, silent testaments to a division overcome and unity restored? The power of that quiet rebellion, the poignant act of reclaiming liberty, resonated deeply.

I remember my children, eyes wide with wonder, bombarding me with questions, their young minds trying to fathom a world divided by concrete barriers and ideological chasms. It was a moment of education, a crossing of generational bridges where history was not just read but profoundly lived and felt.

As the wall crumbled, so did the ideological bastions of the Cold War. Each piece of fallen concrete symbolized hope, a world stepping tentatively yet resolutely towards unity, echoing the silent aspirations of millions who dared to envision a world where divisions were bridged, and humanity prevailed.

The fall of the Berlin Wall wasn't a distant geopolitical event; it was a universal dance of liberation echoing within the silent, sacred spaces of the human spirit. As I hope it did for many, it reminded me that concrete and ideological walls are transient. The essence of unity and freedom endures, echoing through generations, a silent testament to the invincible power of the human spirit to transcend, unite, and forge ahead.

PERSONAL MEMORY PROMPTS ON WORLD STAGE

Reliving Global Historic Moments Together

We've just revisited pivotal moments on the world stage, each echoing the complex and multifaceted narrative of our shared history. Now, it's your turn to dive into the depths of your memory, to awaken the slumbering recollections of days gone by. These prompts aren't just a bridge to your past—they're an invitation to revive the emotions, reactions, and reflections embedded in your life's story. Please share them with friends and family and watch as each answer sparks a cascade of memories, bringing generations together in the timeless dance of storytelling. Every voice adds a unique tone, every memory a vibrant hue, collectively creating a vivid mural of our lived history. Dive in, reminisce, and let the journey of remembrance begin!

1. Echoes of the Korean War (1950s):

Close your eyes and travel back to the 1950s. What images, sounds, or emotions resurface when you remember the Korean War? Did it touch your family or community directly?

2. The Space Race Begins (1957):

Cast your mind back to the launch of Sputnik. How did you, your family, or your school react to this moment? Was there excitement, anxiety, or a mix of both?

3. JFK's Assassination (1963):

Where were you when you heard the news of President Kennedy's assassination? Can you recall the emotions that flooded you or the atmosphere in your surroundings?

4. Civil Rights Movement (1960s):

Reflect on the civil rights era. Were any marches, speeches, or moments left a lasting impression? How did it shape your understanding of equality?

5. Apollo 11 Moon Landing (1969):

Relive the day humans first walked on the Moon. Where did you watch it? How did it make you feel about humanity's potential and the universe beyond our world?

6. Watergate Scandal (1970s):

Bring yourself back to the unraveling of the Watergate scandal. How did it impact your trust in political institutions or shape your view of politics?

7. Oil Crisis (1973):

What changes did you notice in your daily life during the oil crisis? Were there long lines at the gas station or conversations around the dinner table about it?

8. Iranian Revolution (1979):

Try to recollect the media coverage or public reactions during the Iranian Revolution. How did it shape your perception of the world's political landscape?

9. Chernobyl Nuclear Disaster (1986):

Bring back the memory of the moment you learned about the Chernobyl disaster. What were your initial reactions and feelings? Did it change your perspective on nuclear energy?

10. Fall of the Berlin Wall (1989):

Transport yourself back to the iconic moment when the Berlin Wall fell. How did you interpret this event at the time? Did you see it as a symbol of hope, the end of an era, or the beginning of a new world order?

AMERICAN DREAM 50S

My Suburban Tale

A Suburban Dream Unfolds
The Quiet Revolution of American Living

In the 1950s, as the world was slowly healing from the scars of World War II, my family, and many others stepped into a new world - the suburbs. We left behind the crowded city for a life where the skies were open and crickets, not city noises, serenaded nights. It was a different kind of magic, a quiet revolution sweeping America.

Similar to others yet uniquely ours, our house was a part of this quiet transformation. The well-kept lawns and the genuine smiles of our neighbors painted a picture of the American Dream we were all living. Every family was carving out its little world amidst this boom of suburban life.

I was just a kid, but the change was exciting and noticeable. The freedom of playing outside until the street lights blinked on, the community spirit where every neighbor knew your name, marked my childhood. It was the post-war economic bloom, and one-third of Americans, including my family, were beginning a new chapter in the suburbs.

Our new home, with its white picket fence, was more than a house; it symbolized safety, peace, and the fulfillment of my father's dream to provide a sanctuary for his family. It wasn't just a move; it was a step into a future where the promise of prosperity and peace replaced the harshness of war. In those quiet streets and friendly neighborhoods, we weren't just living but weaving the narrative of the iconic 1950s American life.

A Shot of Hope

The Day Polio Lost its Grip (1955)

I was 12 years old in 1955, and back then, summer wasn't just a season of vacations and play; it was also a time of palpable fear. Polio lurked in the background of our joys, an unseen enemy stealing children's laughter and leaving silence and empty desks. Like millions across America, my parents lived in quiet terror, a fear spoken in hushed voices.

On an ordinary day that year, an extraordinary announcement changed everything. Dr. Jonas Salk introduced the polio vaccine with his brilliant mind and compassionate heart. I remember sitting in our living room, the black and white television broadcasting the good news. It was as if someone had flung open the windows of every home in America to let hope breeze in.

I recall the lines that formed in schools, the anxious yet eager faces of parents, and the gentle hands of nurses. One by one, we kids rolled up our sleeves. It was a pinch, a sting, and a collective breath of relief we didn't know we were holding.

The polio vaccine didn't just inoculate us from a crippling disease; it ushered in an era of trust in science and collective action. Dr. Salk handed back our summers, freed our parents from a shadow of dread, and turned fear into a fading memory. Did you know Dr. Salk opted not to patent the vaccine? He was a man who placed humanity over profit, a gesture that amplified the magnitude of our victory over polio.

When Magic Came to Life
The Dawn of Disneyland (1955)

I was twelve when a sprinkle of fairy dust and the wave of an imaginative wand transformed a quiet corner of Anaheim into the happiest place on Earth - Disneyland. I remember it was a buzz amongst all my friends. Though I didn't witness the grand opening in person, the marvel traveled through the flickering screen of our television, and the images of that enchanted kingdom were imprinted in my young mind.

Every kid in America, it seemed, was bewitched. Walt Disney didn't just open gates to a park. Still, he unleashed a universe where fairy tales danced freely amidst the reality of post-war America. I still recall the first time I saw the Sleeping Beauty Castle, not through my eyes, but vividly portrayed in the colorful descriptions of a cousin lucky enough to be among the first to enter that magical realm.

The Sunday evenings after that were marked by Walt Disney's television show, a window into that magical world, making every child a part of his enchanted kingdom. We were transported to frontier lands and future worlds from the comfort of our living rooms. The spark of Disneyland illuminated our young worlds, rendering every obstacle a dragon to be slain and every dream a castle to be built.

Did you know the price of admission on opening day was $1? Even a kid could scramble together, making the magic accessible and the fairy tale not just viewed but lived. Every character, ride, and parade threaded the great American narrative of boundless possibilities and unrestrained imagination.

Rising Voices - The Swell of Feminism in the 1960s

As a teenager entering adulthood, the 1960s were marked by vibrant, passionate, and often tumultuous energies. One of the most profound movements sweeping through the streets, colleges, and households of America was second-wave feminism. I vividly remember the women around me, including my sisters, echoing a newfound voice, a harmonious chorus of courage, demanding equality and respect.

I was too young to grasp the intricate ideologies but mature enough to feel the intense emotions pulsating through the air. Women's roles were metamorphosing, as did the dynamics within our home. I recall my sister Alice balancing her studies with her engagements in rallies and meetings, voicing concerns over issues like workplace discrimination, reproductive rights, and gender equality. An enigmatic energy of change encapsulated her, representing thousands of women nationwide.

We lived through iconic moments, like the passage of the Equal Pay Act in 1963, a beacon of legislative change illuminating the path for women's rights. I still remember the heated, hopeful, and sometimes conflicted dinner table discussions, reflecting a nation wrestling and embracing change simultaneously.

Did you know the 1960s feminism wave was intertwined with other civil rights movements? It was a symphony of liberation, with harmonies of racial, gender, and sexual orientation equality, each amplifying the other. We weren't just witnessing history; we were the raw, unfiltered strands contributing to modern America's intricate, beautiful mosaic. Every rally attended, every article read aloud, and every debate engaged was an addition to the fabric of a more inclusive, equitable nation.

Euphoria in Bloom

The Essence of the 1967 Summer of Love

1967 was a sonnet of freedom, a symphony of colors and sounds that danced gracefully through the air, stitching itself into the fabric of American culture. At 24, the world was an enchanting maze of endless possibilities, and the "Summer of Love" was our playground.

I can still feel the refreshing gusts of wind, heralding a season where love was the currency and peace our anthem. Our small town, usually a sanctuary of tranquility, hummed with a different vibrancy, echoing the distant drums of San Francisco's Golden Gate Park. Each melody, pulsating with youth's raw, unfiltered energy, was a bridge to a world where boundaries dissolved and spirits soared.

Dressed in tie-dyed shirts, a canvas of swirling colors, each hue a silent testament to our quiet rebellion, we were more than observers. We were a chorus of diverse yet unified voices singing ballads of freedom. The flowers blooming in our hair were not mere accessories but symbols of a conviction that love could usher in an era of global harmony.

Every strum of guitar strings wasn't just music but a soul-stirring narrative of a generation unafraid to challenge the status quo. Among the less-known anecdotes is the local 'Peace and Love' gathering we initiated, drawing inspiration from the distant Haight-Ashbury district. It wasn't just a celebration but a statement, a proclamation of our unwavering belief in the power of unity.

The Birth of Titans

Dawn of the Super Bowl Era (1967)

In 1967, as the echoes of the Summer of Love still hummed in our ears, another kind of excitement brewed in the air. At 24, I found another passion that would unknowingly become a lifelong affair - the inauguration of the Super Bowl. Every huddle and tackle on that crisp January day was history.

Gathered around our modest television set, with antennas tweaked for the best reception, my friends and I were enraptured. The Green Bay Packers and the Kansas City Chiefs weren't just teams but gladiators in the arena, embodying America's raw, unyielding spirit. Each touchdown was celebrated with loud cheers in living rooms nationwide, including ours.

Did you know the first Super Bowl wasn't even called the 'Super Bowl'? It was the AFL-NFL World Championship Game. 'Super Bowl' was a term coined informally, inspired by the "Super Ball," a popular kid's toy of the time.

That day, as we witnessed the Packers claim victory, the crowd's roar from the television set was an anthem of a new era. In those exhilarating moments, we were united, not just by a game, but by an experience that would transcend time, evolving into a legacy celebrated by generations to come.

A Sea of Stars and Stripes

The Bicentennial Bash (1976)

The summer of '76 wasn't just any summer. The air was different, with a collective spirit of celebration, nostalgia, and overwhelming pride. I was 33, and though I'd seen many a Fourth of July, nothing compared to this grand spectacle. This wasn't just America's birthday – a 200-year jubilee, a monumental commemoration of our Declaration of Independence.

Every corner of the country was adorned in the iconic red, white, and blue. My family and I joined the sea of patriots, each of us a tiny star in the vast constellation of the American populace, coming together to revel in two centuries of liberty. Fireworks painted the skies, illuminating the dark and highlighting our shared journey as a nation.

On television, the tall ships sailed into New York Harbor, an awe-inducing spectacle that transported us back to the times of our forefathers. It was a harmonious blend of past and present, a time of reflection, and an optimistic gaze into the future. Did you know that every U.S. naval ship entered New York Harbor on that unforgettable day, and more than 200 ships from other nations joined to demonstrate global unity? This wasn't just a national anniversary but a recognition of the American journey, a narrative woven with the threads of perseverance, ingenuity, and the unyielding spirit of freedom.

The Alaskan Pipeline Miracle

A Journey Through Time"

In 1977, the completion of the Alaskan Pipeline marked a pivotal moment in history. I vividly recall the excitement and awe that swept through our nation. It was more than just an engineering feat; it was a testament to human determination, resilience, and ingenuity.

As a child, I remember hearing about the audacious plan to transport oil from the Alaskan wilderness to the southern United States. The idea of a pipeline stretching over 800 miles through rugged terrain and extreme weather seemed like a fantasy. But gradually, it became a reality.

The pipeline brought economic opportunities, transforming remote Alaskan towns into bustling communities. It provided jobs for thousands and fueled dreams of prosperity. Yet, it also ignited environmental debates, with concerns about its impact on the pristine Alaskan wilderness and wildlife.

Politically, it was a hot topic, with debates in Congress and protests in the streets. It was a time when our nation grappled with balancing economic growth and environmental preservation.

One little-known fact is that the pipeline was partially constructed above ground to protect the fragile tundra below. It was an innovative solution that showcased the blend of technology and environmental responsibility.

The Alaskan Pipeline symbolizes what we can achieve when we come together to overcome challenges. It's a story of progress, filled with hope, controversy, and dreams of a better future.

Joysticks & Pixels

The Birth of the Video Game Craze

In the late '70s, a new type of buzz electrified the air. It wasn't the hum of a new hit single or the chatter about a blockbuster film - it was the beeping and blooping of something new: video games. They were born and bred in the iconic arcades and became the sanctuaries of teenagers and adults alike.

I was in my thirties, and you might think that would make me immune to the pull of these pixelated wonders - but oh, how wrong that assumption would be. Even with children of my own, the allure of games like Pong and Space Invaders knew no age limits. Arcades, previously domains of pinball machines, were now aglow with the colorful screens of video games.

I remember the first time I held a joystick, the coarse square edges pressing into my palms, the red button begging to be pushed - it was a new world. The pixeled ball bounced back and forth on the screen, a digital duel of reflexes and reaction, simplicity yet mesmerizing. It's a memory as vivid as my first drive-in movie.

Did you know Pong was inspired by table tennis? And it was deemed so addictive that it broke within days of its initial installation because it was overloaded with quarters? Back then, we didn't just see the birth of video games; we witnessed the inception of a cultural phenomenon that would stretch its pixelated fingers into every corner of the globe.

THE PIVOTAL 80S

My Echoes of Triumph and Tragedy

The AIDS Crisis

A Journey Through the Heartache of the 1980s

The 1980s marked a decade of profound change and turmoil, none more poignant than the emergence of the AIDS crisis. I vividly recall the fear and uncertainty that gripped our nation and the world.

In those early years, AIDS was a mysterious and terrifying illness. Rumors and misinformation spread like wildfire, adding to the confusion. It was a time when ignorance fueled discrimination, and those affected often faced isolation and stigma.

Like many others, my family grappled with the fear of the unknown. We watched as friends and loved ones fell ill, their lives forever altered. It was a time of heartbreak and mourning as the world struggled to understand this devastating disease.

But amidst the darkness, there were glimmers of hope. Communities came together to support those affected by AIDS, and activists fought tirelessly for awareness and research funding. Little-known fact: the iconic red ribbon, a symbol of AIDS awareness, was first worn at the Tony Awards in 1991.

The AIDS crisis was a pivotal moment in history, revealing the best and worst of humanity. It taught us compassion, resilience, and the importance of scientific research. It's a chapter in our history that reminds us of the power of unity in the face of adversity.

Rise of the Machines

My Journey into the World of Personal Computing

In the early 1980s, I, born in 1943, witnessed a revolution that would forever change our lives: the rise of personal computing. It was a time of wonder and excitement as these mysterious machines began to find their way into American households.

Like many others, my family welcomed our first personal computer with curiosity and trepidation. It was a marvel, a box of endless possibilities, and a puzzle with cryptic commands. Learning to navigate this new frontier was like embarking on a thrilling adventure.

As the years passed, personal computers became integral to our daily routines. They transformed how we communicated, worked, and played. We marveled at the birth of the internet, a global web of information that connected us in unprecedented ways.

Little-known fact: the world's first website went live in 1991, created by British computer scientist Tim Berners-Lee. It was a humble beginning for what would become a digital revolution. Personal computing was a technological leap and a gateway to a new era of innovation and entrepreneurship. Startups like Apple and Microsoft became household names, shaping the future of technology. The rise of the machines was not without challenges, but it was a time when we embraced the unknown with open arms. It's a story of how technology became an inseparable part of our lives, bringing both exhilaration and transformation.

Challenger Tragedy (1986)

A Painful Pause in Our Cosmic Odyssey

Born in 1943, I've witnessed remarkable moments in space exploration, but none as heart-wrenching as the Challenger tragedy 1986. It was a day that etched itself into our nation's collective memory.

As we gathered around our televisions, full of anticipation, the launch of the Space Shuttle Challenger was meant to be a triumph, carrying the first civilian teacher, Christa McAuliffe, into space. The excitement was palpable, but it swiftly turned to shock as we witnessed the devastating explosion just 73 seconds after liftoff.

The pain was not just for the loss of seven brave astronauts but also for the shattered dreams of a nation. Little-known fact: The disaster led to a suspension of the Space Shuttle program for over two years as NASA investigated and implemented changes.

The Challenger tragedy forced us to confront the fragility of human endeavors in the vastness of space. It reminded us that, even in our quest for the stars, we remain bound by our humanity. We mourned as one, and it spurred introspection on the risks and rewards of exploration.

In sorrow, it became a moment of unity, reflection, and a renewed commitment to the spirit of exploration. The Challenger tragedy will forever be a solemn chapter in our cosmic journey, reminding us of the sacrifices made in the name of discovery.

PERSONAL MEMORY PROMPTS ON NATIONAL NARRATIVES

A Stroll Down America's Memory Lane

We've walked through significant moments of history together in the previous chapters. Now, it's time to dive deeper and make it personal. These prompts are your gateway to travel back in time, to relive and share the stories close to your heart. Each question leads to a treasure trove of memories waiting to be rediscovered and shared.

So, let's jog those memories and revisit the days that shaped us.

By sharing these stories, we connect, understand each other better, and see the bigger picture of our shared history. Let's dig in and make the past come alive again!

1. The Suburban Bloom (1950s):

Do you remember the first time you saw a sprawling suburb, those perfectly lined homes and gardens? Paint a picture of that moment. What emotions did the new scenery evoke?

2. Polio Vaccine (1955):

Recall the relief and hope that surged when the polio vaccine was introduced. Were you or someone close affected by polio? Share the story of that transition from fear to hope.

3. Disneyland's Magic (1955):

The gates of Disneyland opened for the first time. Did you visit, or did you dream of it? Describe the magic and wonder it inspired in your young heart.

4. Feminist Wave (1960s):

Every wave creates ripples. How did the second-wave feminism touch your life or the women around you? Were there conversations at the dinner table about it?

5. Summer of Love (1967):

Colors, music, love – 1967 was iconic. What are your most vivid memories of this era of freedom and expression? Did you own a piece of psychedelic art or attire?

6. Super Bowl's Kickoff (1967):

Football and fervor! Do you remember the first Super Bowl? Who were you cheering for, and how did you celebrate the grand event?

7. Arcade Games (1970s):

The blips and beeps of the first mainstream video games were mesmerizing. What was your high score, and which game was your battleground?

8. Bicentennial Celebrations (1976):

Fireworks and ardent patriotism. Can you recall where you were during the grand 200th-anniversary celebrations? Paint a picture of the scenes and the air of unity.

9. AIDS Crisis (1980s):

A crisis that shook the world. Share a memory of how the news of the

AIDS epidemic reached you. How did it change the conversations and attitudes in your community?

10. Challenger Tragedy (1986):

A moment frozen in time. Where were you when the Challenger tragedy occurred? Describe the emotions, the silence, and the collective mourning that followed.

THROUGH THE EYES OF A NATIVE SON

My New York Chronicles

I was born into the rhythm of New York's heartbeat, where the towering skyscrapers kissed the heavens and the streets, alive and buzzing, narrated tales of dreams, aspirations, and the undying spirit of a city that never slept. Every corner, every street, and every neighborhood was a world unto itself, in which the rich mix of cultures, histories, and interwoven stories echoed.

Between Two Worlds: A Dance of City Lights and Suburban Stars:

In the post-war grace of the 1950s, I found a different kind of playground - the serene and sprawling landscapes of the suburbs. We'd left behind the towering skyscrapers and bustling streets of New York for a life marked by open spaces and a slower, more tranquil pace. Yet, the city lingered in me, its echoes reverberating in my memory, painting vivid strokes of a childhood marked by urban wonders.

Weekends and holidays were special - we'd journey back to the city's grandeur on those days. I remember the anticipation, the thrill that buzzed in my veins as the familiar skyline came into view. The brownstones of Brooklyn, though no longer home, still echoed with the laughter and stories of a younger me. Neighbors, still as warm and familiar, welcomed us back into the fold, if only for a day or two.

Every visit was a dance between two worlds - the peaceful embrace of suburban life and the electrifying pulse of the city. In those journeys, I discovered the multifaceted soul of New York. This city could be both relentlessly energetic and tenderly nostalgic.

The Transformation:

As the decades rolled, so did the transformation of New York. The 60s ushered in a vibrancy teeming with the effervescent energy of change. The air was thick with the melodies of emerging music genres, the clamor for civil rights, and the audacious spirit of the youth. I witnessed the metamorphosis, where tradition and innovation danced a harmonious ballet, birthing a new era of cultural renaissance.

Turbulent Yet Resilient:

The 70s and 80s brought their share of trials. New York, with its invincible spirit, faced economic hardships, crime, and unrest. Yet, amidst the challenges, there lay an unyielding resilience. Neighborhoods rallied, the cultural scene boomed, and iconic landmarks like the graffiti-adorned subway trains became symbolic of an unbroken city that rose from its ashes time and again.

A Melting Pot of Wonders:

Diversity was the city's crown jewel. Each neighborhood, from the artistic enclaves of Greenwich Village to the vibrant streets of Harlem, hummed a distinct melody, contributing to the symphonic harmony of

New York. Iconic events like the Stonewall Riots were not just local occurrences but monumental moments that rippled through time, echoing the city's ceaseless fight for equality and justice.

The City That Breathes:

I often stroll through the city, a silent observer, watching New York breathe, live, and transform. It's a living entity, a testament to the unwavering spirit of its dwellers, and a narrative of triumphant and tragic historical events. The resilience, the celebrations, the protests, the innovations - every event, every moment is a stitch in the intricate quilt of New York.

Your Turn:

Now, it's time for your narrative. Every town and every city has its unique symphony of stories. What are the memorable moments that shaped your locale? Who were the unsung heroes, the local legends that left an indelible mark on your community?

Dive deep into your memory. Let it be the bridge that transports you back to the turning points, events, and transformations that marked the evolution of your hometown. Share these tales and let them become the strands that knit our collective narrative, deeply personal yet universally resonant.

The Rise of the New York Yankees Dynasty

In the blossoming years of my adolescence, the name 'New York Yankees' was not just a baseball team. It was an anthem of triumph, a narrative of legends scripted under the starry skies of Yankee Stadium. The victories of 1950, '51, '52, and '53 were not just statistics; they were chapters of an unfolding epic, each game, each win, weaving the legacy of a dynasty.

I remember the nights when Dad would take us to the games. The air was thick with excitement, the stadium - a sanctuary where legends walked, and heroes played. Every swing of the bat, every pitch, every catch was a symphony of athletic prowess. We were spectators and witnesses to history, breathing the same air as Yogi Berra and Joe DiMaggio.

With every win, the Yankees engraved their legacy into the annals of sports. And I, a teenager stepping into the dance of youth, was learning lessons not taught in classrooms. In the echoing cheers of the crowd, the triumphant roars filling the New York air, I understood the silent, potent dance between talent and tenacity, dreams and destiny.

The Magical Victory of Roger Bannister

I was just an eleven-year-old boy when Roger Bannister made history. It was 1954, a year that danced with the excitement of post-war promise, and there, amidst it all, stood Bannister - as resolute as a soldier, as graceful as a dancer. I can still remember the gathering around our small living room radio, the anticipation like electricity in the air, a dance of particles buzzing, alive.

The crackling voice of the commentator broke through, echoing in the silence of our living room, where even breaths seemed to be held captive by the moment. My parents, sisters, and I were spellbound as if witnessing a magical event unfolding. Bannister was not just a runner; in that moment, he was every dream unfulfilled, every hope unmet, a symbol of conquest against the insurmountable four-minute barrier.

As the report of his triumphant finish cascaded through the airwaves, a shiver ran through us. "3 minutes 59.4 seconds!" the announcer's voice bellowed. A new world record, a mythical boundary breached. Bannister's strides were not just on the track but also in our hearts, instilling in me a belief that impossibilities were merely constructs of the mind.

Banister's victory was more than a sports achievement for a child whose world was as small as the playground and as vast as the sky. It was a beacon illuminating the path of potential, the untapped and the yet-to-be. Every sprint I ran, every race I won, in the grassy fields of my school, carried the silent chant - if Bannister could, so could I.

The Birth of the NBA Legends

As the fifties unfurled its narrative, another stage of legends was emerging. It was the dawn of icons, where players like Bill Russell stepped onto the court, not just to play but to etch the beginnings of an enduring legacy. I was a teenager, my heart full of unuttered dreams, my spirit pulsating with the untainted optimism of youth.

Each game unfolded as a vivid collage of skill and precision, a dance of defense and offense, amplified by the echoing cheers of captivated audiences. Basketball emerged as a narrated ballet, where each dribble, each leap, and each score painted a vivid story of ambition and triumph.

I would gather with friends, our eyes wide, hearts beating in the rhythm of the dribbles, as we watched the spectacle unfold on the small screen of our black and white television. We were not merely witnesses to games but participants in the birthing saga of legends.

Bill Russell was a harbinger of an era where skill met spirit, where the court became a canvas of athletic artistry. In those tender years of teenage discovery, amidst the silent tumult of adolescence, the NBA became more than a league - it was a silent companion, a narrator of tales where heroes weren't born but made, where legends lived not in the stars but in the quiet, persistent pursuit of greatness.

TRIUMPHANT 60S

My Iconic Matches

The Miracle of the 1960 Winter Olympics

The winter of 1960 was painted with the hues of youthful dreams and silent aspirations. I was 17, my heart a mix of adolescent invincibility and the hushed awakenings of adulthood. Amidst this dance of transitions, the Winter Olympics in Squaw Valley unfolded like a grand spectacle. It was a narrative of human spirit and tenacity.

The USA ice hockey team's victory wasn't just an athletic achievement but a miracle sculpted in ice and snow. We heard the commentary over the radio, the excitement palpable, a collective breath held in anticipation. Every goal scored was a crescendo of euphoria, every defense a silent testament to the unyielding human spirit.

I saw my father's eyes gleam with patriotism and human admiration. In those cold yet heartwarming winter nights, a silent lesson was etched - victories aren't scripted in strength but in spirit, not in the body's prowess, but the soul's unyielding resilience.

Brazil's Glory in the 1962 FIFA World Cup

In the summer of my nineteenth year, amidst the silent transition from adolescent wonders to adult responsibilities, the world paused to witness magic. The FIFA World Cup was a stage where nations met, and narratives of legendary feats were woven. Brazil - a name, an anthem of footballing glory, echoed in the silent corridors of history and the boisterous streets of celebration.

Pele, not just a player but a poet of the football field, painted masterpieces with every touch of the ball. I remember watching, with friends whose names and faces are now etched in the sepia tones of memory, as goals were not just scored but crafted, the artistry that transcended the physical realms into the echoing halls of immortality.

As Brazil lifted the cup, a cheer erupted in our small living room. In that moment of collective celebration, borders, and boundaries melted; we were not just individuals but a part of the pulsating rhythm of a shared human story - scripted not in languages or dialects but in the universal, unspoken language of passion and triumph.

The Unforgettable Rumble of Muhammad Ali

By 1964, I was transitioning from the world of a carefree teenager to a young adult. The spring air was not just a change of seasons but a silent witness to the evolution unfolding within me. In the backdrop of civil rights movements and space races, there was a man, a fighter, echoing a generation's silent rebellions and aspirations. Muhammad Ali - a name that wasn't just heard; it was felt.

The year was marked by Ali's bout with Sonny Liston. I remember gathering with my friends, our young eyes glued to the television. Every punch and every move was a narrative of struggle and triumph. We watched, not just with our eyes but with our burgeoning souls, each jab Ali threw echoing the silent punches life threw at us.

The victory was not just Ali's; it was ours. As he stood there, the world champion, a 22-year-old man with the world at his feet, we, too, felt invincible. Every dream seemed achievable, every aspiration within reach. Ali taught me the dance between vulnerability and invincibility. As we celebrated the victory that night, a silent belief was birthed - we were the architects of our destinies.

GOLDEN 70S

My Heroic Sports Era

The Thrilla in Manila: Ali vs. Frazier

1975 was a year of transformation within my life and across the broader world stage. The winds of change were tangible, and every breath seemed to usher in a new era of awareness. I had become a parent, and my perspective and priorities were shifting. Amidst these personal metamorphoses, the world witnessed a clash of titans, the "Thrilla in Manila."

Ali and Frazier, names as familiar in households as family members, were etching history with their raw power and indomitable spirits. I remember huddling with my loved ones, our gaze fixed upon the television, each punch resonating viscerally. It was more than a boxing match; it embodied human tenacity, the echo of two spirits locked in an unforgettable dance of defiance. Every jab and every knock resonated, not just in the physical space of that living room but deep within our souls. It was a lesson in resilience, an understanding that life's battles, like Ali and Frazier's, were won not just with power but with an unyielding spirit.

Nadia Comăneci's Perfect 10 (1976)

In the middle of the decade, as I juggled the challenges and wonders of parenting, the world stopped to witness perfection, not as an abstract concept but personified in a 14-year-old gymnast - Nadia Comăneci. I can still recall the silence, the collective breath held, as Nadia danced between the bars, a symphony of grace, strength, and perfection.

Every movement was poetry, every leap, a dance between earthly existence and ethereal aspirations. As a young parent witnessing a child achieving the epitome of excellence, I felt both awe and introspection. Nadia wasn't just scoring a Perfect 10; she reminded the world of the unscripted, untapped potential within the human spirit.

In that moment of collective awe, my living room walls seemed to dissolve, and the world, with all its divisions and differences, stood united in admiration of a universal narrative of excellence.

The Pittsburgh Steelers Super Bowl Dominance

The late 70s was a time of transition. My children were growing, and with each passing day, the reflections of their emerging identities painted vivid imageries of tomorrow's promises. In these years of personal thoughts and evolutions, the Pittsburgh Steelers were an anthem of collective resilience and triumph.

Four Super Bowl wins in six years - it was more than a statistic. Each victory was a narrative. Each play was a silent verse of a ballad that echoed a generation's collective aspirations and triumphs.

In the echoing cheers and shared celebrations, there wasn't just the glory of a team's victory but the silent, unutterable testament of a generation that knew the dance between struggles and successes, defeats and triumphs. The Steelers narrated our unscripted yet profoundly real ballads of existence in their iconic play.

TELEVISED 80S

My Sporting Spectacles

Martina Navratilova's Wimbledon Dominance

As the 1980s unfurled its wings, I was deeply immersed in the throes of mid-life. It was a dance between past achievements and future aspirations. Amidst this dance, Martina Navratilova graced the world with a performance that would echo through the annals of time. Every summer, like a cherished ritual, our family would gather, eyes fixed on the television, to witness a woman redefine mastery, making the grass courts of Wimbledon her sanctuary.

Martina's grace was not just in her skilled shots or unyielding endurance. It lay in her ability to weave magic under pressure, to sculpt poetry amidst intense competition. Each stroke and victory was a testament to a woman's journey of unwavering determination and raw skill.

Our children, now entering their teenage years, watched with widened eyes, absorbing a champion's techniques and spirit. For them and us, Martina's triumphs were lessons, silent yet profound, about the power of resilience, the magic of self-belief, and the endless beauty of striving.

Diego Maradona's 'Hand of God'

1986 brought with it a moment that would be forever etched in the collective memory of sports enthusiasts. Our family sat glued to the television, hearts pulsating with the rhythm of the FIFA World Cup. In this electrifying atmosphere, Diego Maradona, with divine finesse, scripted history with the 'Hand of God.'

It was a goal that transcended the defined boundaries of a football match; it was art, controversy, and the epitome of human ingenuity. We reveled in heated discussions, our living room echoing with voices dissecting the moment with analytical precision yet tinged with awe.

Maradona's iconic goal was a victory narrative, but it also touched upon the grey shades of human ingenuity. It was an unscripted lesson for our young ones on the complexities of life's stage, where victory, ethics, and brilliance often danced in an intricate ballet.

The Rise of Air Jordan

Michael Jordan's Entry into the NBA

As the decade neared its twilight, a new star ascended, illuminating the basketball courts with an ethereal glow. Michael Jordan was a name that would become synonymous with unmatched skill and unyielding spirit. As parents of young adults now, witnessing Jordan's rise was akin to watching the birth of a legend.

Our family, like millions globally, watched in awe. MJ was not just playing basketball but crafting a narrative of boundless possibilities, an anthem of hope and unparalleled skill.

In those evenings, there was an unspoken realization as the sun bowed to the moon and the echoes of Jordan's triumphs resonated in our space. We were not just witnesses to a player's journey but participants in the collective celebration of human potential, unbridled, untethered, and eternally glorious.

PERSONAL MEMORY PROMPTS ON SPORTING EVENTS

A Sprint Through Sports History

We now step into the roaring stadiums and echoing halls where legends were born, and history was made in real time. Sports, more than any other activity, has the power to unite diverse crowds in collective celebration. Every goal scored, every record broken, every triumphant cheer holds within it the shared heartbeat of millions. These prompts are your ticket to a grandstand view of those unforgettable games and iconic athletes that defined the spirit of each decade. Whether you were a passionate spectator or a dedicated player, each question is tailored to usher you back to the electrifying world of victories, near misses, and the undying spirit of the game. Dive deep, reminisce, and may each memory unlock and bring back the rush of those golden days!

1. Golden Games Reflection

Take a moment to reminisce about a significant sporting event from your past. It could be the thrill of a World Series game, the excitement of a Super Bowl, or the elegance of the Olympics. What were you doing at the time, and who were you with? Jot down the emotions that surged through you and how that event influenced your perspective on sports.

2. My First Live Match

Remember the first time you attended a live sports event? Who were the teams playing, and who took you there? Describe the atmosphere, the roars of the crowd, and the colors that filled the stadium. How did this experience kindle or enhance your love for the sport?

3. Epic Victories and Crushing Defeats

Recollect a time when you were wholly engrossed in a game, and the outcome had you leaping with joy or sinking in disappointment. How did this emotional roller-coaster enhance your connection to sports? What conversations and debates did this spark among your friends and family?

4. Sports and Family Traditions

Many families have sporting traditions, like watching the big game together, playing in the backyard, or attending local matches. Share memories of these cherished times. What snacks were a must-have? Were there any special rituals or superstitions adhered to during significant games?

5. Iconic Athletes of Your Time

Think back to the sports legends of your youth and adulthood – those athletes who were more than just players but icons who left an indelible mark on the sport's history. Write about your favorite athlete, the memorable moments they gifted fans, and how their performances stirred emotions and inspired conversations in your home.

HEADLINES OF THE 50S

My Inception in a Changing World

The Coronation of Queen Elizabeth II

A New Era for the British Monarchy

1953 ushered in an event that stitched its eloquence not just in the grand annals of British history but in the shared narrative of the world. I was a 10-year-old boy, and the coronation of Queen Elizabeth II was a spectacle of magnificence that danced vividly before my eyes, a mix of tradition, dignity, and grace.

As did millions globally, our family sat huddled around the radio, ears attuned to every word as if each syllable echoed the heralding of a new era. Even in my tender years, the gravity of the occasion was palpable, the silent acknowledgment that history was being written, and we were the silent witnesses of its majestic dance.

Every description painted by the eloquent narrators was a brushstroke of an unfolding masterpiece, the emergence of a queen who would become emblematic of steadfastness and dignity. Though separated by an ocean, the echoes of that ceremony reverberated in our little living room in New York, and the vast expanses of the Atlantic seemed to dissolve, uniting us in a moment of collective awe.

The Discovery of DNA

Cracking the Code of Life

In the spring of 1953, amidst the bloom of flowers and the soft hum of life reawakening, another form of awakening unfurled. Watson and Crick's discovery of the DNA's double-helix structure was less of a scientific revelation and more of a cosmic unveiling. I was a lad of ten, yet the ripples of that discovery swept across the world, touching the shores of understanding with a silent yet profound eloquence.

My father read the newspaper aloud in the evenings, articulating the realms of a hidden world now exposed. This mystique air would fill our living room. We were not just a family nestled in the heart of New York but silent participants in humanity's grand odyssey of discovery.

The revelation of DNA was like lifting a mystical veil, exposing the intricate dance of life's creation. Each evening, as discussions around the discovery filled our family space, the walls of our modest home seemed to expand, giving way to the infinite expanses of the universe and the intimate corridors of human existence. We were witnessing a moment where science, mystery, and the profound eloquence of life's composition met. In that intersection, the silent echoes of awe were birthed.

The Launch of Barbie Dolls

A Cultural Phenomenon Begins

1959 painted a memorable chapter in my youthful years. Amid adolescent explorations and naive aspirations, a distinct creation graced the world. The launch of the Barbie doll became an indelible part of my generation. I was a 16-year-old, consumed by books and the era's music. Yet, Barbie's entrance was like a magical whisper of a different world, brushing against the corners of our youthful dreams.

I remember my little sister, eyes wide with the sparkle of fascination, clutching her first Barbie doll, an emblem of a modern fairytale. Though I was edging towards the tumultuous seas of adulthood, witnessing her joy, a blend of innocence and thrill, was profoundly stirring. It wasn't just a doll but a symbol of imagination, aspiration, and the unseen threads weaving the dreams of countless young souls.

As the years unfolded, Barbie wasn't confined to the playrooms but echoed the evolving roles of women in society. Every new edition was a silent testimony to the changing tides, the subtle yet profound transitions painting the canvas of the time. It was an epoch where the boundaries were expanding, and every Barbie held in the tender hands of a child was not just a toy but a silent whisper of the infinite horizons that lay ahead.

THE DEFINING 60S

My Witness to Epochal Events

The Invention of the Laser
Lighting Up Future Technologies

1960 brought the whisper of the future into the present with the invention of the laser. Aged 17 and immersed in the wonders of science at school, this revelation was akin to stepping into the pages of a science fiction novel, where the boundaries between the conceivable and the fantastical blurred.

The laser was not just a technological advancement; it was poetry in motion, a dance of light that held promises of transformation beyond comprehension. Discussions with classmates, the animated exchanges with teachers, every conversation was tinged with a silent awe, a reverence for an invention that held the seeds of future revolutions.

The laser symbolized limitless potential in the tender space where youth was giving way to adulthood. It epitomized the conviction that we were on the brink of an era where the light wasn't just illumination but a vessel of untold innovations, carrying within its beams the echoes of future symphonies of progress.

The Introduction of the ZIP Code

Organizing America's Mail

1963 was when the simplicity of numbers metamorphosed into a system of profound organization - the introduction of the ZIP Code. I was navigating the complexities of a college education then, every letter from home a cherished artifact of love and belonging.

The ZIP Code was not just about order; it was a bridge that transformed distances into touchpoints of connection. Each code was a silent bearer of narratives, every parcel, and letter, now a part of a precise, swift dance of communication.

In the subtle silences of nights spent in books, the arrival of a letter marked with the distinct ZIP Code was a whisper of an evolving world.

It was a testament to the fact that amidst the rapid strides of technology and innovation, the intimate touch of handwritten letters was preserved and enhanced. In those codes lay the silent echo of a world becoming smaller, where distances were not measured in miles but in the swift, quiet journey of letters that found their way home with precision and warmth.

The Installation of the 911 Emergency System A Lifesaving Innovation

In 1968, an evolution in public safety unfolded before our eyes. I was 25, freshly graduated, and the world's energy was teeming with a blend of revolutions and changes. The installation of the 911 emergency system was one such stride that marked its significant print on the epoch. Every number dialed was a summoning of immediate assistance and prompt response in times of distress.

I can still recall the moment's gravitas, imbued with a newfound assurance that help was just a call away. As a young adult venturing into the world's vastness, with parents growing older, this innovation wasn't just technological but profoundly personal. It was an unspoken solace, a silent guardian that watched over our lives.

Conversations at the dinner table ventured into imaginings of a world where assistance, hope, and help were now measured in mere minutes. It unified communities and families, instilling a sense of collective security. We were no longer isolated entities but parts of a woven fabric where every thread was reinforced by the silent yet vigilant presence of 911.

PROGRESSIVE 70S

My Innovative Horizons

The Proliferation of Video Games

The Launch of Pong

By the time the 1970s rolled around, I was a settled family person with kids who were as curious about the world as I was in my youth. 1972 marked the arrival of Pong, a technological marvel that would change our living room dynamics forever. The simplicity of two paddles and a bouncing ball on our television screen transformed ordinary evenings into electrifying tournaments of joy and laughter.

I remember the glow in the kids' eyes, the gleeful shouts, and the joy that filled our home. We weren't just witnessing the birth of video games; we were part of a generation dancing on the cusp of a digital revolution. Each bounce of the pixelated ball was a leap into an era where technology and entertainment would meld into inseparable entities.

Those evenings, hands wrapped around the rudimentary gaming console, we weren't just playing a game. We were scripting memories of when the digital age was in its infancy, innocent yet awe-inspiring. Pong was a prelude to a symphony of technological wonders that awaited us.

The Introduction of the UPC Barcode

Revolutionizing Retail

In the mid-70s, another innovation subtly yet profoundly changed our lives. Introducing the UPC barcode turned mundane trips to the grocery store into an experience of efficiency and wonder. I recall the fascination, watching items swiftly scanned, each beep a testament to an age where commerce and technology intertwined seamlessly.

It wasn't just about the speed of checkouts or the efficiency it brought; it was the realization that we were stepping into a future where technology infused simplicity and organization into every facet of life. The children, wide-eyed, would watch the cashier with keen interest as each beep marked the transition from manual to mechanical, old to new.

In those bar lines and numbers, we saw a future of unison, where every product and item was part of a global lexicon, understood and recognized universally. The barcode was a universal language that transcended borders and dialects.

The First Test Tube Baby

A Medical Milestone

1978 brought whispers of miracles not in realms of divinity but in the meticulous hands of science. Louise Brown, the world's first test-tube baby, was born. A medical marvel that defied norms and ushered humanity into an age where life's genesis could be witnessed beyond the natural womb.

In the quietness of our home, with the children safely tucked into bed, my spouse and I would discuss the profound implications. We were in an era where science was no longer just an observer but a creator, a gentle weaver of life's sacred tapestry.

Every news broadcast, every headline that chronicled this marvel, was a reminder of the delicate dance between ethics, progress, and possibilities. We witnessed an epoch where every advancement carried the solemn echo of human potential and the profound responsibilities it invoked. Our children were growing up in a world where the miracles of science weren't just observed but lived every day.

DYNAMIC 80S

My News Chronicles

The Debut of CNN
The 24-Hour News Cycle Begins

In 1980, the news and information landscape was about to be revolutionized. In the stillness of our living room, with the glow of the television illuminating the faces of our now almost-grown children, we witnessed the inception of CNN, the world's first 24-hour news channel. The unassuming buzz and hum of the television set, a familiar backdrop to our family's evenings, was suddenly charged with a new energy.

Every headline, every story, now had an immediacy, a pulse. The world felt closer, more tangible. The stories weren't just read; they were experienced. Our children, on the brink of adulthood, bore witness to this shift with eyes wide with curiosity and wonder. They were stepping into a world where information was available, alive, breathing, and constantly evolving.

I recall the awe that danced in their eyes, reflections of a world expanding, bursting at the seams with stories told in real time. A luxury we hadn't realized we were missing until Ted Turner's vision brought the world to our doorstep. Amidst the Cold War's ending whispers and technology's loudening voice, we sat together as a family, participating in a real-time global narrative unfolding. CNN was a bridge connecting us, and millions worldwide, to a reality where stories weren't just told but were lived, moment to moment.

The Release of the Rubik's Cube

A Puzzle Craze Sweeps the Globe

1980 also unveiled another iconic gem that would nestle itself into the fabric of our family's recreational hours - the Rubik's Cube. This colorful, puzzling masterpiece brought an effervescent joy, illuminating our evenings with lively challenges and triumphant victories.

I remember the laughter and the playful competition around the dining table. With nimble fingers and minds ablaze with possibilities, our children ventured into the maze of colors and patterns. Each twist, each turn, was a dance of intellect and intuition, a colorful ballet where minds, young and old, met and marveled.

Erno Rubik's creation wasn't just a puzzle; it symbolized an era where complexities and wonders coexisted, where problems, though intricate, were solvable. Each solved cube in our household was a testament to patience, resilience, and the joyous celebration of small victories amidst life's grand ballet.

The Popularization of the Camcorder
Personal Video Recording Becomes a Reality

As the 80s progressed, another marvel of technology graced our lives - the camcorder. We were no longer mere observers of time; we became its chroniclers. Every birthday and milestone was now captured in the silent, still frames of photographs and the living, breathing, moving images and sounds.

I can still feel the camcorder's weight in my hands, an extension of our desires to hold onto moments slipping away in time's relentless march. Our children's laughter and the tender moments of familial love now had a permanence, a sanctuary in tapes that would bear witness to time's passage.

Our children, now stepping into the world as young adults, were captured in these frames, immortalized in their youthful exuberance. We were storytellers, weaving narratives of ordinary moments graced with extraordinary love. Every tape, every recording, was a chapter of a story that was and is perpetually unfolding - a testament to a time when technology gifted us the means to be the narrators of our epics.

PERSONAL MEMORY PROMPTS ON NEWS HEADLINES

Unfolding the Pages of History

As we sift through the annals of history, we see that each headline holds a universe of stories, emotions, and reflections. These major news reports aren't just words printed on a page or flashed across a screen but powerful markers of our collective journey. They have shaped our perspectives, stirred our emotions, and influenced the world we navigate today. Each news event offers a mirror reflecting the global narrative and our personal stories - where we were, what we were doing, and how these moments impacted our lives. These prompts invite you to step back and unravel your memories intertwined with these significant headlines, igniting a soulful exploration of the past's profound touch on your present.

1. A Headline to Remember

Reflect on a newspaper headline or news report etched in your memory from your younger days. It could be a historical event, a shocking revelation, or a joyful announcement that gripped the nation. How did you come across this news, and how did it impact you and your loved ones?

2. The Stories That Shaped Us

Each era is marked by significant news stories that influence the collective consciousness. Choose a news event from each decade of your life and write about where you were, who you were with, and how it shaped your worldview. Did it bring about any changes in your everyday life or long-term plans?

3. The Day the Earth Stood Still

News events are so monumental that they make the world stop in its tracks—everyone remembers where they were and what they were doing. Recall such an event in your lifetime. Describe the atmosphere, the people's reactions, and how it made you feel.

4. Technological Tidings

Innovations and technological advancements have always made headlines. Think back to a piece of technology that was introduced and shook the world with its invention. How did you first hear about it, and what were your initial reactions? Did you embrace it immediately, or were you skeptical?

5. A Personal Connection to Global News

There are global events that, even though they might be happening miles away, resonate on a personal level. Recall a news story that, for some reason, felt personal to you. Write about how you heard the news, your initial reactions, and how it affected your life, conversations, and perspective in the subsequent days.

Chapter 3

Invention and Innovation

THE DAY MY WORLD DANCED TO PROGRESS

I still remember the crackling sound of the radio broadcasting Elvis Presley's latest hit as Mom prepared breakfast on that radiant summer morning of '55. Our cozy kitchen, with its well-worn countertops and familiar aromas, was a sanctuary of warmth and family unity.

The change began with the arrival of our first refrigerator - a gleaming, hulking miracle of modern convenience that replaced our trusty old icebox. I recall my sister's wide-eyed wonder and Dad's proud smile as we marveled at the shelves, brimming with fresh produce, milk, and leftovers that were no longer subject to the whims of melting ice.

As Presley's voice echoed the excitement of a new era, our kitchen embarked on its revolution, too. The introduction of the electric dishwasher was nothing short of a revelation. Once raw and weary, Mom's hands found respite, and the clinking of dishes became a symphony of progress.

Yet, the automatic washing machine signaled the dawn of a new age. Saturdays, once earmarked for the tedious ritual of laundry, were transformed. I recall the inaugural hum of the machine, a sound that ushered in weekends of family outings and leisure, unburdened by the shackles of domestic toil.

Every appliance brought a slice of the future, a promise of ease, and a dance of progress. With its soft, assuring hum, the air conditioning unit turned sweltering summers into seasons of comfort. We gathered around, basking in the cool air, a family united by blood and the shared transformation journey.

As I stroll down this memory lane, I realize that each appliance, every hum and buzz, is not just a testament to technological advancement but a chapter of our family saga. It wasn't just our kitchen that was transformed but our lives – woven into the fabric of an era where technology and humanity danced to the jubilant tunes of progress and possibility.

OF WHEELS AND WINGS
MY SOARING JOURNEY

The echoes of post-war triumph still hummed in the air as I, a child of the '50s, stepped into a world where wonders were not confined to imaginations but sprung to life around us. My father, a prominent engineer, was the harbinger of prosperity to our family. With his steadfast hands, he weaved structures and laid the foundations of a life where boundaries were meant to be nudged.

A Chevy, A Family, and Open Roads

The Chevrolet Bel Air was our chariot of freedom. I still remember the sparkle of its curves under the golden sun; it wasn't just a car but a ticket to uncharted territories. Every weekend was an expedition, every road a narrative of discovery as our family of four explored the sprawling beauty of New York and beyond.

First Flight: An Unforgettable Ascent

But amidst the revving engines and open highways, a golden opportunity arose—a journey not across lands but skies. Flying was a symbol of luxury in those days. However, our family was stepping into the aircraft's aisle thanks to Dad's accomplishments. It wasn't an ordinary day but a momentous occasion—Grandma's 70th birthday on the distant shores of California.

I remember my first flight: the thunderous roar of the engines and the graceful ascent into the clouds. It was magic - a dance between earth and sky.

I was a bundle of nerves and excitement. The cabin, a capsule of wonders, hummed with an energy, an echo of the revolutions of the propellers cutting through the skies. I remember pressing my little nose against the window, eyes wide, as the vast expanse of America unraveled below - mountains, rivers, the patchwork of states - a geography lesson painted in the vibrant strokes of reality.

As the engines hummed and the plane began to ascend, I was gripped by anxiety and exhilaration. The city below gradually transformed. I was leaving the world I knew and venturing into the heavens, a realm previously reserved for birds and celestial bodies.

I had the window seat, a privilege that made me the family's appointed narrator of the world above. The clouds weren't just masses of water vapor but mystical entities, canvases on which my imagination painted stories of distant worlds and magical beings. Each cloud held a shape, a narrative, transforming the journey into a silent movie scripted by nature.

My parents, seated beside me, exchanged amused and endearing glances. To them, the journey was as much about witnessing my wonder as it was about the flight. My mother's hand found mine, a gentle touch that spoke the language of silent reassurance and shared awe.

A stewardess with a beaming smile offered candies - a ritual, she explained, to ease the ear pressure. But to me, it was a gift from the heavens, a token from a journey where the skies weren't a limit but a beginning.

Every cloud we sliced through, and every city we soared over encapsulated the realization of the American Dream in our family's narrative.

The Transformation of Journeys

The journey was more than a flight; it was an emblem of our family's ascent. The strides of technology have leaped not just into the spheres of the public but also into the intimate corners of our lives. Every trip in our cherished Bel Air, each flight, was not just a physical journey but an exploration of the evolving American Dream—a dance of possibilities and realities.

The Apollo Impact

The Apollo 11 Moon Landing in '69, the iconic moment when man first kissed the lunar surface, was not a distant spectacle but an intimate experience. Gathered around the television, each image of astronauts imprinting the lunar surface echoed the imprints of progress in our lives.

The Evolution Continues

The '70s and '80s unveiled another chapter; cars weren't mere vessels of travel but artifacts of elegance, embodying generational aspirations. The evolving designs mirrored our metamorphosis, each model more sophisticated, echoing the relentless stride of a nation and a family towards uncharted frontiers.

A Reflection

As the wheels turned and the wings soared, every journey was a chapter inscribed in the silent annals of our family's journey. We were not mere witnesses to the dance of innovation but active participants, our lives echoing the rhythmic strides of a world stepping unfalteringly into tomorrow.

In this dance of progress, from the mesmerizing hum of the Bel Air's engine to the serene glide amidst the clouds, technology wasn't an external entity but a silent companion of our lives—each journey a harmonious blend of human touch and mechanical grace, a narrative where boundaries were not just pushed but lovingly, triumphantly, dissolved.

FROM LETTERS TO KEYBOARDS
MY EVOLUTION WITH WORDS

When I was a kid, writing letters by hand was the norm after World War II. I remember sitting at the kitchen table, a piece of paper in front of me and a pen in hand, carefully crafting messages to relatives and friends.

In our family, letters were special. Each word was chosen carefully, and it felt like a piece of the sender's soul was in every message. I remember the neat writing on the pages of the letters we would receive, each one a treasure of words and emotions.

Then came the '60s, and the telephone took center stage with them. It was amazing to pick up the receiver and hear the voice of a loved one instantly. Our living room became a place where we would gather for calls, and voices filled our home, making distances feel short.

But change didn't stop there. In the '70s and '80s, something new came along - computers. I recall the day we got our first one. It was a mix of excitement and mystery. With computers came emails, a way to send messages worldwide in the blink of an eye.

Typing my first email was a memorable experience. The words appeared on the screen as my fingers danced on the keyboard, and with a press of a button, the message was sent. It was fast and convenient, but I couldn't help but miss the personal touch of handwritten letters.

Seeing how we moved from writing letters to sending instant emails is impressive. Each step was like a new chapter, showing how far we've come. Even though technology made things faster and easier, I sometimes miss the slower, more personal touch of the older ways. Each handwritten letter was unique, carrying a piece of the person who wrote it.

PERSONAL MEMORY PROMPTS

Technological Trips Down Memory Lane

Let's take a moment to look back on how technology has changed our lives. These questions will help you remember the gadgets and inventions that were a big part of your world. Think about your first TV, car, or computer - what was it like? How did you feel? Please share your stories and take a trip down memory lane with me. Each memory is a piece of a bigger picture, showing how we all grew and changed with the world around us.

1. A New Dawn in the Kitchen:

Do you remember the first modern appliance your family brought into the home? Share the excitement and how it changed your daily routines.

2. Family Road Trips:

Reflect on a memorable family journey made special by a car. How did the open roads feel, and what adventures awaited?

3. Taking Flight:

Can you recall the first time you ever boarded a plane? Describe the emotions and the sights from your window seat.

4. Ring, Ring Goes the Telephone:

Share a story of when a phone call brought your family joy, surprise, or even shock. How did the instant connection impact your relationships?

5. Your Computer Chronicles:

Take a trip down memory lane to the day the first computer entered your home. What were your first impressions, and how did you adapt to the digital age?

6. From Pens to Keyboards:

Share the emotions and adjustments you experienced transitioning from handwritten letters to emails. Do you miss the personal touch of a penned note?

7. Magical Machines:

How did household innovations, like the washing machine or microwave, affect your family's lifestyle? Share a story of the day-to-day transformations.

8. Journeys Unleashed:

Recount a memorable journey that was made possible or significantly enhanced by technology. How did it change your perception of travel?

9. Email Epiphany:

Share your memories of sending your first email. How did it feel to communicate instantly, and how did it change your correspondence habits?

10. Tech-Enhanced Bonds:

How has technology strengthened your relationships with distant friends or family? Share stories of connections revived or maintained thanks to these innovations.

Chapter 4

The Feel of the Times

In this chapter, we'll revisit the emotions stirred by unforgettable personal and shared moments. Each section opens a window to a different scene - the universal pulse of emotions, the color and spirit of local and national celebrations, and the tender, intimate memories of family life. Each memory is a strand, intertwining to create the rich fabric of our collective journey. Dive in, and you may see reflections of your experiences echoing back.

IN THE MIDST OF EMOTIONS

My Sentimental Stride

Curiosity: The Mystique of Area 51

I was a young adult, fresh out of high school and stepping into the world with eyes wide and mind curious when whispers of Area 51 first tickled my ears. It was the late '50s when every child looked up at the stars with wonder and anticipation. We were a generation raised on the thrilling tales of Jules Verne and H.G. Wells, and the notion of life beyond Earth wasn't just a possibility; to us, it felt like an impending reality.

One evening, as I huddled with friends around a flickering campfire, Jimmy – the adventurous among us – spun the tale of Area 51. Nestled deep in the Nevada desert, shielded by the enigmatic embrace of the sand and stars, it was said to harbor secrets of extraterrestrial encounters. Jimmy spun tales of unidentified flying objects, eerie lights painting intricate dances across the desert sky, and meetings that defied explanation and ignited imagination.

Years turned into decades, and the mystery around Area 51 thickened. Every new account, every whisper of alien technology and classified experiments, stirred a persistent and unquenchable curiosity. We knew the moon's barren landscape, but what about the enigmatic confines of our Earth?

Even in the golden years of my life, the allure of Area 51 remained, a veiled and vibrant chapter in American history. The U.S. government's acknowledgment in 2013 wasn't a revelation but a confirmation of the silent symphony of questions that had lingered for decades. Area 51, with its ethereal enigma, wasn't just a geographical location but a testament to the insatiable, glorious curiosity that defines the human spirit. Every story, every supposed encounter, wasn't an end but a beguiling continuation of a narrative as boundless as the universe itself.

Shock: The Twist Takes the Stage (1960)

I was a tender 17 in 1960, when our collars were still starched, and dance floors were places of elegance and finesse. Each movement and each step was a dance of grace and restrained beauty. We were a generation standing on the precipice of change, yet still nestled in the traditions handed down to us.

One evening, amidst the croons of Sinatra still lingering in the air, something unprecedented struck the sanctified silence of my small town. The radio, our window to the world, trembled with a new sound and rhythm - it was Chubby Checker's 'The Twist.'

Oh, it wasn't just music. It was a storm, a whirlwind that whipped through our quiet lanes and peaceful evenings. I remember the first time I saw 'The Twist' in action. The town hall had transformed from a place of modest hops and waltzes into a tumultuous sea of swirling bodies and unbridled energy.

Our feet, accustomed to the gentle sways of ballroom dances, were now agents of rebellion, breaking every rule we'd ever known. Parents and elders looked on in a mix of horror and fascination. It was shocking in its purest form. A cultural electric jolt marked the departure from the old world into something wild, untamed, and thrillingly uncertain.

It wasn't just a dance but a declaration of a generation that was no longer content to follow. We were ready to lead, to make our own rules. Checker's voice, pulsating through the airwaves, wasn't just sound. It was the echo of change, the anthem of a youth ready to twist away from the old, to a beat all their own, into a future where the shackles of convention lay broken amidst the jubilant steps of the liberated.

Inspiration: The Peace Corps Establishment (1961)

In the early 60s, as a young adult stepping fervently into the enthusiasm of life, I witnessed an event that stirred the nation and ignited a spark within me. It was 1961, a year marked by the vibrant energy of President John F. Kennedy, a leader who embodied youth, hope, and invigorating change.

I can still recall the palpable excitement that tingled in the air when Kennedy announced the establishment of the Peace Corps. The television set, our window to the world, brought JFK's fervent speech into our living room. He spoke of peace, extending hands of friendship across borders, and the need to understand and be understood. It wasn't a call to arms but to serve, bridge divides, and foster global unity.

Imagine the thrill! The possibility of venturing beyond the familiar terrains of our hometowns to lands distant and diverse, cultures enigmatic yet enchanting. Every volunteer story was a testament to the transformative journey that lay ahead. We weren't just witnessing history; we were invited to be part of it.

Did you know that over the ensuing decades, more than 235,000 volunteers would step into 141 countries, weaving relationships that transcend politics and borders? In those early days, we didn't just see it as an adventure but a calling. The Peace Corps was more than an organization; it was a movement, an ethos. In the eyes of a young man, every announcement of a new volunteer setting foot in another land was a narrative of inspiration, a testament that we, too, were global citizens. Our world, once defined by the boundaries of states and nations, was expanding, and we were stretching our arms, ready to embrace it all.

Pride: The Establishment Of Environmental Protection Agency – Epa (1970)

In the late autumn of 1970, I was finding my footing in a changing world. I'd survived the turbulent '60s with its blare of rock 'n' roll and the challenges and triumphs of the civil rights movement. It was a time when we looked at the world around us with awe and skepticism. We'd sent a man to the moon, yet our beautiful American landscapes were threatened here on Earth.

I remember thumbing through the morning newspaper. The headlines were usually filled with the Cold War's latest. Still, this particular morning, a different headline caught my eye. President Nixon had just announced the establishment of the Environmental Protection Agency - the EPA. It struck a chord with me. I'd grown up admiring the sprawling beauty of our nation, from the misty mountains to the golden plains and the sprawling cities in between.

We'd built, innovated, and transformed, yet smokestacks clouded the skies, and rivers bore the stains of progress. The creation of the EPA wasn't just another government announcement. It signified a turning point for millions of others and me - an acknowledgment that the land we loved deserved our respect and care.

I recall a neighbor, old Mrs. Thompson, always used to say, "We borrow this Earth from our children." The establishment of the EPA brought those words to life. The nation was taking a collective step, not just in advancing industry and technology but in the stewardship of our natural inheritance.

It was a point of pride. We were a nation capable of monumental achievements in science, music, and culture and one attuned to the silent plea of our rivers, forests, and skies. We were maturing, and the seeds of environmental consciousness were sown in that evolution. Who could forget the first Earth Day, just a few months before the EPA's inception? A day of unity, awareness, and a shared commitment to safeguarding the beauty that defines our American soul.

Wonder: The Concorde's First Flight (1976)

I watched in astonishment as the Concorde took its first transatlantic flight in 1976. I was in my thirties then, and I remember that day like yesterday. As this gleaming symbol of human achievement soared through the skies, the world seemed to hold its breath. It crossed the Atlantic in under four hours, half the time it took a regular airliner.

I wasn't on that historic flight, but I vividly recall sitting in front of the television, eyes glued to the screen, as news anchors, with barely concealed excitement, reported live on this monumental event. The Concorde was a beacon of human ingenuity, a tangible testament to our relentless pursuit of pushing boundaries and conquering frontiers.

Each sonic boom was a magnificent display of speed but a reminder of how far we had come since the days of the Wright brothers. I remember conversations with friends and family, all of us marveling at a world where the skies were not just crossed but conquered with unprecedented speed. Little known to many, the Concorde's distinct pointed nose could be moved, a design innovation to allow pilots better visibility during takeoffs and landings. This incredible machine could reach speeds of over 1,300 miles per hour. It was a marvel of human engineering and a source of national pride for the British and French teams that designed it. As I looked up at the sky that day, the Concorde etched a luminous arc against the azure expanse, encapsulating a moment where anything seemed possible. It was an era where our aspirations were not just reaching for the skies but surpassing them, where the dance between human aspiration and technological innovation waltzed gracefully into the annals of history.

Hope: The Launch Of Voyager 1 (1977)

At 34, the earth, with its familiar landscapes and predictable rhythms, had etched a comfortable, yet somehow confining, existence for me. The world, though vast, had limits, boundaries that whispered of the finite and the knowable. But in 1977, as autumn painted the skies with transition hues, something magnificent pierced through the earthly restraints.

Voyager 1, a crafted symphony of metal and intellect, soared beyond our world, heralding an era where the stars weren't just distant flickers of light but reachable, tangible entities. I remember gathering around the old television set, its screen flickering with the ghostly images of a rocket ascending through the atmosphere and the constraints of our collective imagination.

Did you know that Voyager 1 carries a Golden Record with it, a time capsule intended to communicate the story of our world to extraterrestrials? In the silent expanse of space amidst galaxies and stars, the sounds of Earth, our music, our voices, our essence, would traverse eternity.

As it slipped through the silken threads of our atmosphere, every image Voyager 1 relayed was a triumph of technology and a whisper of infinite possibilities. With its wars, successes, and tribulations, Earth was a pale blue dot in the vast cosmic arena.

In that moment, watching that piece of human ingenuity travel where no man ever had, a profound sense of hope bloomed. We weren't just inhabitants of Earth but cosmic entities woven into the very fabric of the universe. In the silent spaces between stars and galaxies, I found the echoes of infinity, an unutterable proof that we, too, were limitless.

Nostalgia: The Release Of 'Grease' (1978)

I was 35 when 'Grease' hit the theaters. Ah, the instant rush of nostalgia, as tangible as the thick, buttery aroma of movie theater popcorn. There it was, the magical '50s, spread out on the big screen in all its whimsical glory. A time machine intricately woven from melody and dance, pulling us back to the era of sock hops and soda shops.

Every scene was a painted picture from my adolescence, and every song was a musical note from the soundtrack of my formative years. Remember how we swayed to the tunes of the jukebox, the clinks of soda bottles underscoring our laughter and dreams?

Did you know that initially, 'Grease' was a raw and aggressive depiction of teen life in the '50s? It was softened for the big screen, turning raucous realities into sweetened memories. It was a gift with a golden hue to those eager to remember the past, where trials were mere stepping stones to jubilant victories.

A bittersweet longing stirred as Olivia Newton-John and John Travolta danced through scenes stitched together from our own lives. We were no longer the kids with rebellious hearts and untamed spirits but adults with responsibilities, seeing our reflections in a mirror tinted with the gentle hues of yesterday.

I walked out of the theater under the starlit sky, the melodies of 'Grease' echoing the harmonious blend of past and present. In the evolving world, amidst the noise of progress, 'Grease' was a gentle whisper, a reminder that though times change, the melodies of our past linger, sweet and eternal.

Fear: Three Mile Island Accident (1979)

In '79, I was firmly in the rhythm of adult life. The woes and wonders of the world, once distant echoes, now resonated loudly, each event weaving itself into the fabric of my daily existence. The Three Mile Island Accident was one such event, a chilling melody of fear that broke the harmonious tunes of my life.

I remember that March morning vividly. The air was still, the skies painted with the soft hues of a promising dawn. But the news spread like wildfire, turning the serene morning into a tumultuous day. A malfunction in the second reactor of the Three Mile Island plant in Pennsylvania – words that invoked a gripping silence, a haunting stillness.

A latent fear resided in our hearts, the shadow of Hiroshima and Nagasaki still looming large. The marvels of nuclear energy, promising yet petrifying, were akin to a dance on the edge of a sword. A power so immense, so unforgiving.

Did you know that the incident released a small amount of radioactive gases, but not enough to cause harm? It's a trivia often lost amidst the throes of panic that enveloped the nation. There were no immediate injuries or discernible health impacts, but the psychological imprint was indelible.

The streets were abuzz with hushed conversations, eyes wide with the realization of our vulnerabilities. Yes, we were advancing, but at what cost? The incident wasn't just a near-miss but a clarion call, a stark reminder of the narrow ledge between progress and peril upon which humanity tread, a silent dance amidst the echoing drums of potential catastrophe.

Resilience: The Recovery From The Oil Crisis (1979)

In 1979, I was well into my thirties and a witness to an era where the world, especially America, was put to a stern test – the oil crisis. The long lines at gas stations, the rationing, and the skyrocketing prices are images etched into the collective memory of a generation. It was a period where the usual hum of cars on the open roads grew silent, and the incredible American journey seemed momentarily paused.

But amidst the challenge, something remarkable unfolded – a testament to the indomitable human spirit. I recall neighbors carpooling, communities coming together, and an echo of unity in times of adversity. It was a period where innovation wasn't just a term tossed around in tech labs but was alive in the daily lives of ordinary folks. We learned to adapt, to conserve, to be mindful.

Here is a little trivia that's often overlooked: During this period, the national speed limit was reduced to 55 miles per hour to conserve fuel. It wasn't just a legal mandate but a symbolic gesture, a nation adapting to the tides of change in unison.

The recovery from the oil crisis wasn't just about stabilizing economies or ebbing geopolitical tensions. It was about resilience, the quiet, unyielding strength that defines humanity. We survived the oil crisis and emerged from it with a renewed sense of our collective power and the subtle realization that adversity, however formidable, was no match for the combined resolve of a united people.

The oil crisis wasn't a period of defeat but a chapter of triumph. It was a narrative of a nation and a world that faced adversity and emerged unbroken and stronger, a testimony to the invincible human spirit in us all.

Joy: The Miracle On Ice (1980)

Ah, the winter of 1980. I was 37, and the world was a different place then. We were in the grip of the Cold War, and every headline in every news bulletin seemed like a constant reminder of the icy relations between our great nation and the Soviet Union. But amid this cold, metaphorical, and literal, there came a moment that warmed the hearts of millions and ignited a blaze of joy that would be remembered for generations.

The Winter Olympics in Lake Placid weren't expected to be a spectacle for us. Our ice hockey team was a young, scrappy bunch, not the seasoned professionals we wished to have in such dire times. The Soviet team? Oh, they were giants, invincible and formidable, each player an epitome of athletic prowess. They weren't just players; they were a reflection of Soviet power.

I remember sitting with my family, eyes glued to our television. It was one of those old color sets where the vibrancy of hues wasn't just seen but felt. The game? Oh, it was less of a match and more of a dance, where each goal and each save was a step, a movement in a ballet of icy elegance.

As the clock ticked down, something miraculous unfurled. The young Americans, our boys, were scripting history on ice. Each goal was like a strike against the cold walls of the political divide. I remember our neighbors' roar and jubilant yells, echoing the sentiments of an entire nation.

When the buzzer marked the end, signaling a win not just for the team but for every American, we were no longer just citizens; we were participants in a 'Miracle.' Political tensions and economic worries were all eclipsed by an all-consuming joy. It wasn't about the Cold War or politics but about that shared moment of unutterable delight, a reminder of our collective spirit that could surmount the impossible.

I remember stepping outside, the winter chill biting yet somehow less cold, less harsh. The stars twinkled a little brighter, echoing the sparkle of the impossible made real. The 'Miracle on Ice' wasn't just a game won; it was a narrative of triumph, a story where every American found a chapter written, not in the annals of history, but in the boundless realm of joy.

INTERACTIVE JOURNAL SECTION

YOUR EMOTIONAL MOSAIC

Now, dear reader, I invite you to embark on a personal journey into the annals of your memories. Draw from the well of the past and relive the emotions stirred by the untold stories and the silent yet significant moments that colored your world.

Amazement: Recall an event or invention filled with wonder and awe. What was unfolding around you, and how did it shape your view of the world?
Apprehension: Were there moments of uncertainty and anxiety triggered by the unknown, change, or mysteries that veiled the future?
Elation: Identify a moment of collective celebration, a victory, or an

achievement that elevated the spirits of a community, a nation, or th[e]
world.

Jot down these intimate narratives, breathe life into the silent echoes of emotions, and unfold the pages of a past that is as personal as it is universal. Each feeling and every memory contributes to the intricate dance of history. The silent yet eloquent steps of your recollections and reflections enrich this dance.

LOCAL FESTIVITIES

My Cultural Immersions

County Fair Memory: A Night Of Enchantment

Back in the golden haze of my youth, county fairs were the epitome of magic. Each was a world, a spectacle of lights, sounds, and emotions that only seemed possible in the most vivid dreams. The Ferris wheel, majestic and glorious, stood as a beacon of awe, its hypnotic lights weaving patterns in the night sky, turning the ordinary into something utterly enchanting.

The air was a symphony of laughter and chatter. A melody spun from the golden threads of community, friendship, and the unspoken bonds that link us all. It wasn't just noise; it was the music of unity, a song that still echoes in my heart's silent, nostalgic chambers.

Every game, every ride at the county fair, was more than a transient jolt of excitement. They were the threads that wove us, a patchwork comof diverse souls, into something resembling a family. We shared ill of victory at ring toss, the exhilarating rush of the roller coast- .d the simple, unadulterated joy of cotton candy melting on our tongues.

Those fairs were chapters of an unwritten epic, each moment a verse, each laughs a chorus, singing the age-old ballad of human connection. In the sea of hypnotic lights and the cacophony of jubilant sounds, we found something profound, something that transcends the ephemeral nature of time – we found each other.

Years have passed, and the world has turned, yet in the silent recesses of my memory, the lights of the Ferris wheel still dance, the laughter still rings, and for a moment, we're all there together, under the starlit canvas of the night, eternal in our transient moment of shared existence.

City Parade Recollection: Unity In Colors

Even after all these years, another memory that shines brightly in my mind is of a splendid city parade that painted our streets with colors and life. Those parades had a certain magic, weaving the entire city into a spell of unity and excitement. As a boy, I remember waking up to the distant sound of drums. This rhythmic calling heralded the day of spectacle and celebration.

Like many kids in the neighborhood, I would jump out of bed and hurry to the sidewalks, eyes wide with anticipation. The parade had a way of turning the ordinary streets into wonder stages. The majesty of the floats, each masterpiece, told stories of our heritage, achievements, and dreams. Every color and every sound felt like it was painting strokes of joy across the city's canvas. One parade, in particular, has never left me.

The theme was 'Unity in Diversity,' every float represented different c tures, creating a mesmerizing mix of human togetherness. The music, a harmonious blend of other tunes, reflected a world where differences danced together in perfect harmony. Each float was a moving piece of art celebrating our shared humanity.

In that tender age, amid the sparkle and fanfare, I grasped a truth that has stayed with me – our differences are not barriers but bridges. They are the colors that paint our world vibrant and beautiful. As the last float passed and the crowd dispersed, a silent pledge was born in my young heart – to embrace, celebrate, and love the diversity that makes us us. In the retreating tunes of the music and the fading lights, that city parade left an indelible print of unity, not just on the streets but in my soul.

NATIONAL CELEBRATIONS

My Patriotic Moments

Stars, Stripes, and Unity

Every Fourth of July, our neighborhood would transform into a living tableau of patriotic fervor. Flags fluttered in every corner, each stripe and star telling its silent tale of liberty. The aroma of barbecues filled the air, signaling a feast that was as much about shared stories as it was about shared flavors. There was an unspoken yet palpable sense of unity.

Kids with faces painted, embodying the spirit of freedom, would dance ıelodies that filled the air. These melodies told stories of brave rs and a nation forged in the crucibles of diversity and democra- he night descended, fireworks lit up the sky. Each burst of color was a testament to a nation's resilient, undaunted spirit birthed from the passionate quest for freedom and equality. On those nights, gazing up at the starlit spectacle, we realized we were not just observers but active participants in our great nation's ongoing, ever-evolving narrative. Every cheer was a pledge to uphold the values that knit us together, a chorus of diverse voices singing a unified anthem of liberty, justice, and the pursuit of a more perfect union.

A Feast of Gratitude

One crisp November afternoon stands out in my memory, painted with the golden hues of a perfect Thanksgiving Day. Our home bustled with activity, the kitchen alive with sizzling sounds and the savory aromas of Mom's legendary roast turkey. Each dish prepared was a labor of love, a culinary sonnet of gratitude.

That year, the table seemed to stretch endlessly, adorned with abundant food. Yet, it wasn't the quantity but the warmth of shared smiles, the clinking of glasses, and the chorus of laughter that made the atmosphere magical. Cousins, aunts, uncles - every face was a chapter in my life's book, every embrace, a reminder of the threads of love and histories that bound us together.

As we bowed our heads for the traditional prayer of thanks, there was a silent acknowledgment of the blessings that graced our lives. The golden turkey with mashed potatoes, each dish was more than a meal – it was a symbol of the harvest of love, resilience, and togetherness we were fortunate to reap. Stories flowed as freely as the wine, and as candlelight danced in the eyes of my loved ones, I was awash with a profound sense of gratitude. In that moment of reflection, I understood that Thanksgiving wasn't merely a day on the calendar but a living testament to the beauty of pausing, coming together, and acknowledging the richness that family and shared memories bring into our lives.

FAMILY TRADITIONS

My Hearth and Home Tales

A Haven Amidst the Pines

The anticipation began weeks before summer, a palpable excitement woven into our daily lives as we eagerly looked forward to the annual journey that meant much more than a vacation - a retreat into a realm where serenity and familial bonds reigned supreme. Every year, as the last school bell heralded the onset of freedom and the city buzzed with the invigorating energy of summer, my family would pack our bags, our spirits high with the promise of rediscovery and bonding. We embarked on our pilgrimage to the old family cabin, a sanctuary nestled amidst the whispering pines. Our cabin was a harmonious blend of old-fashioned charm and raw nature. The aged wooden beams, each telling a silent tale of the generations that sought refuge within its welcoming confines, held within them a legacy of family narratives, echoing laughter, whispered secrets, and quiet reflections. Nestled by the river whose gentle murmurs accompanied our nights and greeted our mornings, this sacred space was untouched by the rapid advancements of the outside ere, amidst the verdant woods and under the watchful eyes of , we were pulled into a more spartan existence where the weavnnections stemmed from shared experiences and intimate exchanges. Every fishing expedition, every meal cooked over the open fire, and every story narrated under the starlit sky added layers of richness to our family narrative. As children, we were explorers in this secluded haven, our days marked by discoveries of hidden trails and secrets that the forest generously unveiled to its cherished guests. As adults, it was a retreat where the noise of our busy lives dimmed and the essential, often overlooked, threads of family and togetherness were lovingly rekindled. Each return to the city marked us with a subtle yet profound transformation, carrying within us the silent songs of the woods, the river's gentle lullabies, and a refreshing sense of connection that only the untouched embrace of nature and the unfiltered communion of the family could bestow. This annual pilgrimage was more than a tradition; it was our sanctuary of rediscovery, a cherished odyssey where the essence of family and the silent, majestic whisperings of nature converged into unforgettable summers.

Christmas in Our Home

The magic of Christmas always painted every corner of our home with splashes of joy and laughter. December was a particular time that weaved our family closer together. The cold air outside was a striking contrast to the warmth that filled our home, created by love and the excitement of the holiday spirit.

Mom was the heart of our Christmas. She had a special touch, turning ordinary decorations into extraordinary displays of beauty and sentiment. Each ornament hung, and every pie baked was a piece of her heart shared with all of us. In those moments, the decorations symb[illegible] family's love and unity.

Christmas morning was a world of wonders. Opening gifts was like uncovering magical secrets; every unwrapped present brought smiles and expressions of surprise. Our Christmas tree, adorned with lights and ornaments, bore witness to these precious family moments.

Then, there was the Christmas feast. We gathered around the table: grandparents, uncles, aunts, and cousins, each adding their unique flavor to the family mix. It was a time when stories flowed, laughter echoed, and connections deepened.

During these magical Christmas times, the world outside stood still. The hustle and bustle of life paused, making room for something far more precious - family, love, and togetherness. Every laugh shared, every story told, under the soft glow of Christmas lights, became ingrained in the ever-growing chronicle of our family's history; these moments lived in our hearts, cherished memories that would warm us for years.

PERSONAL MEMORY PROMPTS

Unearthing Treasured Memories

We each hold a rich mosaic of memories assembled from the pieces of grand and intimate moments. Yet, these precious recollections sometimes lay dormant, waiting for the gentle nudge of reflection to bring them to the surface. These carefully crafted prompts are your keys to unlocking those hidden treasures. Embark on a journey through time

p into your reservoir of memories. Revisit the laugh-
derie, and the silent, profound moments that define the
ur experiences. Whether it's the infectious energy of local
ades, the solemn pride of national celebrations, or the warm embrace of family traditions, each question is a doorway to a world where the past lives and breathes. Step in and reacquaint yourself with the intrinsics of your stories, crafting a narrative as unique as the journey you've traversed.

1. Festive Atmosphere:

Recall a local festivity that you attended. What sounds, sights, and smells surrounded you? Try to bring to mind the sensory details that made the event unforgettable.

2. Community Bonds:

Think back to a town parade or a county fair. Who were you with? Tell how the event fostered a sense of community and belonging.

3. Iconic Events:

List some annual local events or traditions. How have they evolved over the years? Are there any particular moments or changes that stand out?

4. Fourth of July Memories:

What is your most memorable Fourth of July celebration? Describe the fireworks, the gathering, and the emotions it evoked.

5. Thanksgiving Traditions:

Remember a memorable Thanksgiving. Who was at the table? Share a story of a particular conversation or incident that occurred.

6. Patriotic Feelings:

Describe an event or moment during a national celebration that made you feel a strong sense of patriotism. What symbols and expressions of national pride were evident?

7. Holiday Gatherings:

Think about your family's unique holiday traditions. What activities, foods, or customs make your family's celebrations distinct?

8. Summer Retreats:

Recall a family vacation or summer retreat. Describe the destination and share a memorable story of what happened during that time.

9. Generational Rituals:

Are there rituals or traditions passed down in your family through generations? Write about how they started and what they mean to you.

10. Special Occasions:

Remember a birthday, anniversary, or another family occasion that was celebrated specially. What made it different and memorable?

Chapter 5

Echoing Through Ages

This chapter closely examines how events, music, and culture from previous decades still touch our lives today. We'll explore the lasting effects of the past and draw direct lines to the present, showing how those moments continue to shape our world. It is a journey of discovery, unveiling the living legacy of times gone by. Join me in connecting the dots between then and now, understanding how we are woven into the ongoing story of our shared history.

THE MELODIES OF YESTERDAY

My Eternal Echoes

Lasting Impact

Sometimes, it feels like history is a treasure trove of moments, each a gem that sparkles with memories. Take rock 'n roll, for instance. Those electrifying tunes that first hit the airwaves in the 1950s didn't just fade away. They're still alive, pumping energy and spirit into the songs we hear today. Every chord and lyric tells a story, capturing the rebellion and freedom of a generation while influencing the music we dance to now. And it's not just music. The milestones that marked our journey, like those iconic steps on the moon or the first buzz of a personal computer turning on, are living memories. They don't just belong to the past; they reach out, touching our lives today, shaping our world, making history a living, breathing story where the past and present meet. Each moment from yesterday has left its mark, creating paths that we walk on today, showing that history isn't just something to be remembered – it's something that lives with us in every note of music, every technological marvel, and every step forward.

Then & Now

There's a certain kind of magic in looking back and seeing how far we've come. I can recall the days when receiving a handwritten letter was a special occasion. Each word inked carefully on paper, carried the warmth and presence of a distant loved one. Today, our world moves at the speed of a click, and emails deliver messages in an instant. It's a contrast that speaks volumes of our journey.

I remember the bulky, black-and-white television sets that used to be the centerpiece of our living rooms. Families would gather around them, tuning in to watch the latest episode of a beloved show. Flat screens with crystal clear images and streaming services have transformed how we watch, what, and when. Yet, that shared joy of witnessing stories unfold on screen, the communal experience of media, remains unchanged.

Cars, too, have come a long way. The vintage models, iconic designs, and roaring engines are far from today's sleek, silent, and eco-friendly machines. We've gone from tuning radios to get the clearest signal of our favorite station to having the world of music available at our fingertips through apps and digital interfaces.

Fashion has its tale to tell. The flared trousers and floral prints of the '70s echo today's revival trends. The style has evolved, but the essence, the expression of individuality, and the cultural currents through attire continue to be a significant part of our identity.

In these comparisons, there's more than just a reflection of technological and cultural evolution. There's a narrative of continuity, a thread that connects the charm and simplicity of yesteryears to the sophistication and pace of today. It's a journey that underscores a fundamental truth - times change, and technologies evolve. However, the core human experiences, the emotions, and the connections they endure link every 'then' to our 'now.'

YESTERDAY MEETS TODAY

My Intergenerational Dance

Now, weave the threads of the past into the present and future fabric. Every family is a living narrative, a dynamic story that every member across every generation shapes. Here, I'll suggest activities and narratives enriched with warmth and wisdom to bridge generational gaps. It's more than a walk down memory lane; it's a passage where generations meet, exchange, and are forever bonded. Join me as we celebrate the beauty of shared histories, the resonance of collected wisdom, and the joy of family bonds that time and distance fail to wane.

Storytelling sessions

Picture this: a cozy evening where the family gathers around, the room imbued with anticipation and warmth. Here, our seasoned family members transform into storytellers, their voices weaving our family history's intricate, colorful narratives. These sessions aren't formal but intimate, personal, and profoundly moving.

Start by creating a comfortable setting. It could be the living room, where old photo albums and mementos can accompany the stories, adding a visual and tactile element to the narration. Light the room softly, perhaps with the gentle glow of a fireplace or some candles, to create a space where the past can dance freely into the present.

Prepare some prompts or themes to help our older gems embark on their storytelling journey. It could be "The Day We Met," "The Hardest Challenge," or "A Lesson Learned." The young ones can play a part, too. Their curiosity becomes the key to unlocking treasured memories, unveiling stories as educative as they are endearing.

Encourage an atmosphere of patience and respect. This is a time for listening, for allowing the echoes of the past to resonate in the silence of the present. There's learning in this silence, a silent transmission of wisdom, values, and family legacy that no book or movie can ever encapsulate.

Remember, every story told, every memory shared, isn't just a nostalgic journey. It's a sacred passage where legacies are handed down, the young absorb the essence of their lineage, and the old see the reflections of their lives in the eyes of those who will carry their stories into tomorrow. Every laugh shared, every tear shed, every tale spun stitches the fabric of a family bound together by blood and shared histories and cherished memories.

Legacy Projects

Legacy Projects offer a beautiful opportunity to intertwine the hands of every generation in the family, working together to create something tangible. This relic speaks of our shared history, values, and stories. It's more than a project; it's a journey of discovery and connection and the creation of something that will be cherished for generations to come.

One profound way to embark on this journey is by creating a family tree. It's a visual, engaging, and enlightening venture. Start by gathering information and delving into the roots, the branches, and the intricate connections that define your family. Involve the youngest to the oldest members, and let each voice, memory, and puzzle piece find its place. You'll marvel at the stories, the histories that unveil themselves, breathing life into every name, every connection etched onto this tree.

Or perhaps dive into the world of photo albums or digital projects. Imagine a book where each page is a portal to a different era, a different memory, embellished with pictures, anecdotes, and the unique touch of every family member. Include photographs, letters, and memoirs – every piece adds a layer, enriching this family treasure. In the digital realm, create a multimedia narrative, weaving videos, audio recordings, and images into an immersive experience of your family's journey through time.

Assign roles based on interest and expertise to make this endeavor more engaging. The tech-savvy youngsters can take charge of the digital aspects. At the same time, our seniors bless the project with the wealth of their memories and stories. Make it a collective effort, where every weekend or family gathering becomes an opportunity to build, share, and connect.

Ultimately, a Legacy Project isn't just about the beautiful family tree that adorns your wall, the richly detailed photo album on your coffee table, or even the digital narrative accessible with a click. It's about the moments created, the stories shared, the bonds strengthened. It's a journey where every step, every story, and every contribution is a testament to the rich, diverse, and beautifully complex entity we call family.

Recipe Sharing

A magical alchemy happens in the kitchen, where ingredients, aromas, and flavors weave together to create more than just dishes but memories, stories, and bonds that linger long after the meal is enjoyed. Recipe sharing is not just about exchanging ingredients and cooking methods but about weaving together the threads of different generations, each adding its unique flavor to enrich the family's shared heritage and traditions.

I recall the heavenly aroma of grandma's apple pie wafting through the house. This scent was as much a part of our family gatherings as the laughter and stories that filled the air. Every recipe and every dish has a narrative, a history laced with memories of family gatherings, Sunday dinners, and special occasions. Each is a precious heirloom, carrying the essence of the family's soul, passed down through generations.

Now, imagine a cozy afternoon where grandma is in the kitchen with the grandchildren, her seasoned hands expertly maneuvering through the process, each step narrated with anecdotes and stories of the past. It's a dance of generations, where the past and the present meet, connecting over the universal language of food. The youngsters bring their curiosity and fresh perspective. In contrast, our seniors bring a wealth of tradition, experience, and stories that turn every recipe into a narrative.

To facilitate this beautiful exchange, designate a 'Family Recipe Day.' Create a space where the old and the young can exchange recipes, cook together, and, most importantly, weave stories and memories into every dish. Let the kitchen be filled with the rich aromas of traditional dishes, each bringing to life the tales of times gone by.

In these shared moments, every stir, every chop, every bake is more than a step in the cooking process; it's a stitch weaving generations together, a blend of the rich legacy of the past and the vibrant energy of the present. As the dishes come to life, so does the family's narrative, each recipe a chapter, each aroma a memory, each flavor a piece of the beautiful mosaic that is our shared family story.

Memory Games

Consider the creation of customized memory card games. I've found that intertwining fun charm with the richness of family and historical memories can be a delightful and enriching experience. Imagine a deck of cards, but not your regular playing cards. Each card is a snapshot of a cherished family memory or a significant historical event, a visual echo of times gone by. Every card flip isn't just a step closer to winning the game but a portal to a precious moment in time, an opportunity to relive, remember, and rejoice in the richness of our shared journey.

Creating this game is simplicity itself. Gather family photos, those treasures that hold within them the silent yet eloquent narratives of days, months, and years passed. They could be photos of Grandpa in his youth, your parents' wedding, or perhaps the first family reunion. Each image is a gem, a piece of the jigsaw that completes the family picture.

Print these photos and adhere them to sturdy card stock, transforming each into a playable card. Mix the cards with significant historical events that family members have experienced or are connected to create a rich and varied combination of personal and shared history.

Now, gather around the table, shuffle the deck, and let the game begin. Each card turned over is a gateway to a story, an invitation to plunge into the depths of memory, share, listen, and connect. The young ones might stumble upon stories never before heard. The elders might find their hearts warmed by the vibrant echoes of the past. Together, every play and every round weaves the past into the present, turning a simple game into an intricate dance of generations, connecting, sharing, and creating memories destined to be cherished forever.

Time-Travel Interviews

Time-travel interviews are a gem of activity, offering a platform for the younger generation to step into the past of their elders, unraveling stories and experiences that shaped them. Imagine this - a cozy afternoon, the family gathered around, the air thick with anticipation and curiosity. The younger ones, equipped with a recorder or a smartphone, are ready to embark on a journey through time, with their grandparents or elder relatives as the trusted guides.

Each question is a gateway to a different era, and every response is a narrative of lived experiences. Perhaps it's about the Summer of Love in '67, the energy of the civil rights movement, or the advent of color television - each story a peek into a world the younger ones have only read about or seen in movies.

But this isn't a one-sided affair. The elders, too, see their world through fresh eyes, recounting their days of youth, the challenges they overcame, the joys they celebrated, and the milestones they witnessed. It's an exchange, a dance of words and memories that breathes life into the black-and-white pages of history, painting them with the vibrant hues of personal experiences.

And as the record button is hit, voices and legacies are captured. These aren't just interviews - they are chronicles of resilience, triumph, love, and evolution, stored for future generations to discover, explore, and connect. In this beautiful exchange, history becomes personal, and the past is remembered, lived, understood, and cherished. Each recording becomes a family heirloom, a precious keepsake that preserves the richness of bygone eras, ready to be revisited and relived.

Movie Nights

Movie nights are an age-old family favorite that effortlessly bridges the gap between generations. But how about adding a nostalgic twist to it? A sprinkling of history, a dash of cultural exploration, and a generous helping of family bonding.

Here's the plan. Transform your living room into a time machine that transports the family to distinct eras with each movie. Select films that are not just cinematic masterpieces but also cultural landmarks, each offering a glimpse into the times in which they were made. From the rebellious spirit of the '60s encapsulated in films like "Easy Rider" to the colorful extravagance of the '80s seen in "The Breakfast Club," each movie becomes a window to a different world.

Now, this isn't just about popping popcorn and enjoying a film. No, it's an experience, a journey. After each film, let the room bloom with conversations. Share anecdotes, exchange perspectives, and delve into discussions. The older members can share their first-hand experiences of those eras, the trends, the triumphs, and the challenges. The younger ones can observe the societal shifts, draw parallels with today, ask questions, and share their reflections.

Movies have this enchanting ability to be both mirrors and windows. They reflect the times they're made in and offer a view into a different world. So, each film becomes a catalyst, igniting dialogues, unveiling memories, and fostering an enriched understanding. It's more than a movie night; it's an expedition through time. It's about seeing the past through the lenses of cinema and conversations in the cozy comfort of your living room, surrounded by the warmth of family.

PERSONAL MEMORY PROMPTS

Bridging Yesterday and Today

As we journey through the echoing paths of the past, these specially crafted prompts serve as gateways to deeper exploration and reflection. They are your invitations to delve into the nostalgia, drawing parallels between the cherished yesteryears and the dynamic present. Through these prompts, embark on a journey of rediscovery, unveiling the enduring imprints of your formative years and the subtle yet profound ways they continue to color your world.

1. Revisiting the Soundscape:

Think back to your favorite songs from the '50s-'80s. How do they compare to the music you enjoy today?

2. Screen Evolution:

Recall the films and TV shows you loved back in the day. How have storytelling and cinematic techniques changed over the years?

3. Style Revival:

Remember the fashion trends during your younger years. Do you see any of these trends making a comeback?

4. Communication Transition:

Compare how you stayed in touch with friends and family in earlier decades to now. What do you miss, and what improvements do you appreciate?

5. Travel Back in Time:

Think about the cars or other modes of transportation you used to own or dream about. How do they contrast with today's models?

6. Political Echoes:

Reflect on significant political events from your youth. How have these shaped your perspectives and the political landscape today?

7. Holiday Memories:

Revisit how holidays like Christmas or Thanksgiving were celebrated in your family. Have the traditions changed over the years?

8. Family Narratives:

Recall family stories or legends that have been passed down. How have these narratives shaped your family's identity?

9. Technology Timeline:

Consider the household appliances and gadgets that were a staple in your home. How does the technology of then compare to what's in use now?

10. Cultural Influences:

Reflect on the cultural movements that you witnessed. How do you see their impact on today's society and youth?

CONCLUSION

An Unending Journey - Where The Past Meets The Present

We've reached the journey's end, a nostalgic sojourn through the echoes of timeless moments, enduring melodies, and personal milestones that still reverberate within our souls. These pages are more than ink and paper; they are a bridge where the silent whispers of yesteryears dance gracefully with today's vibrant rhythm.

In this shared odyssey, we brushed against intimate recollections and monumental eras, revealing that we are not mere spectators of time but active narrators. Each story and each memory contributes to an enduring legacy, a continuum linking the past's rich narratives with today's unfolding tales and tomorrow's uncharted adventures.

As this chapter concludes, let the harmonious echoes of the past enrich your present, each note, and narrative a guiding light illuminating paths ahead. May these recounted histories linger, fostering reflections and dialogues that transcend time.

As you linger on the final page, envision a horizon where memories and promises converge, each sunrise heralding tales yet unveiled. In this eternal dance of time, every moment is a precious stitch in the grand narrative of life, waiting to be woven with grace, wisdom, and an enriched spirit.

Thank you for walking this path with me and finding echoes of your journey mirrored in these stories. Until our paths converge again, treasure each unfolding chapter. Farewell, and onward to horizons yet discovered.

APPENDICES

QUIZ ZONE

Test Your Memory

Welcome to the Quiz Zone, where memory and fun intertwine! This section is your playground to reminisce about the moments covered in the book and other iconic instances that have left an indelible mark on our lives. Each question is crafted to take you on a diverse journey, exploring the grooves of classic tunes, the magic of unforgettable movies, and the pulse of historical events. Whether you've walked through the pages of this book or are simply a lover of the echoes of the past, there's something here to spark those cherished recollections. Enjoy!

MULTIPLE CHOICE QUESTIONS:

1. Which Beatles album, released in 1967, is considered one of the most influential in music history?

A. Help!

B. Abbey Road

C. Sgt. Pepper's Lonely Hearts Club Band

D. Rubber Soul

2. Who was the first man to walk on the moon in 1969?

A. Alan Shepard

B. Buzz Aldrin

C. Neil Armstrong

D. Michael Collins

3. Which invention revolutionized home entertainment in the 1950s?

A. Personal Computer

B. Color Television

C. Video Cassette Recorder

D. Microwave Oven

4. What annual event celebrates the signing of the Declaration of Independence?

A. Memorial Day

B. Veterans Day

C. Independence Day

D. Labor Day

5. In which decade did the rock 'n' roll genre first become popular?

A. 1940s

B. 1950s

C. 1960s

D. 1970s

6. Which invention became popular in households during the 1980s and revolutionized how people listened to music?

A. Vinyl Records

B. Cassette Tapes

C. CD Players

D. Track Tapes

7. Which historical event led to the national holiday, Veterans Day, celebrated on November 11th every year in the U.S.?

A. The end of World War II

B. Signing of the U.S. Constitution

C. The end of World War I

D. The signing of the Declaration of Independence

8. Which event of the 1980s symbolized the end of the Cold War?

A. The Vietnam War's End

B. The Fall of the Berlin Wall

C. The Gulf War

D. The Space Shuttle Launch

9. Who was the U.S. President during the first moon landing in 1969?

A. Richard Nixon

B. John F. Kennedy

C. Lyndon B. Johnson

D. Gerald Ford

10. Which music festival, held in 1969, became a pivotal moment in the history of music and is remembered as an emblem of the counterculture era?

A. Lollapalooza

B. The Monterey Pop Festival

C. The US Festival

D. Woodstock

FILL IN THE BLANKS QUESTIONS:

1. The ______ Brothers were a famous comedy team known for their rapid-fire puns and slapstick humor in the 1950s.

2. In 1963, Martin Luther King Jr. delivered his famous "I Have a ______" speech, a pivotal moment in the Civil Rights Movement.

3. The first man-made satellite, ______, was launched by the Soviet Union in 1957.

4. In 1971, Walt Disney World opened in ______, Florida.

5. The ______ Crisis in 1962 brought the U.S. and the Soviet Union to the brink of nuclear war.

6. In 1979, the United States faced a __________ crisis, marking a period of fuel shortages and long lines at gas stations.

7. The ______ parade is a popular New Year's Day event in Pasadena, California.

8. In 1980, the United States boycotted the Summer Olympics held in ______.

9. The iconic _________ was a significant part of family living rooms, showcasing memorable events and offering a glimpse into worlds far from home.

10. In the 1950s, families gathered around the television set to watch ______, a popular variety show.

MUSIC AND MOVIE QUIZ QUESTIONS WITH MULTIPLE-CHOICE ANSWERS

1. Which song features the lyrics, 'Just a small town girl, living in a lonely world'? Can you remember where you were when you first heard it?

A. "Born to Run" by Bruce Springsteen

B. "Sweet Child o' Mine" by Guns N' Roses

C. "Don't Stop Believin'" by Journey

D. "Hotel California" by Eagles

2. Identify the movie where a young man lifts a boombox over his head outside a girl's window, playing a romantic song. What were you doing around the time this movie came out?

A. "The Breakfast Club"

B. "Say Anything..."

C. "Pretty in Pink"

D. "Ferris Bueller's Day Off"

3. Name the song that begins with 'I've paid my dues, time after time.' Can you recall when this song played a backdrop to your life?

A. "Imagine" by John Lennon

B. "Bohemian Rhapsody" by Queen

C. "We Will Rock You" by Queen

D. "We Are the Champions" by Queen

4. Which movie, set in the disco era of New York, starred John Travolta as a working-class young man who spends his weekends dancing? How did this film impact your nightlife?

A. "Footloose"

B. "Saturday Night Fever"

C. "Dirty Dancing"

D. "Flashdance"

5. This movie quote, 'Life is like a box of chocolates, you never know what you're gonna get,' is from which iconic film? How did this quote resonate with you?

A. "The Shawshank Redemption"

B. "Forrest Gump"

C. "Pulp Fiction"

D. "The Godfather"

6. Which movie featured the song “Don’t You (Forget About Me)” during its opening and closing credits, becoming an anthem for teen films in the 1980s?

A. “Pretty in Pink”

B. “Sixteen Candles”

C. “The Breakfast Club”

D. “Ferris Bueller’s Day Off”

7. In which movie does the character Johnny Castle say, “Nobody puts Baby in a corner”? Reflect on where you were or what you did when this film was released.

A. “Pretty Woman”

B. “Footloose”

C. “Dirty Dancing”

D. “Top Gun”

8. In the iconic dance movie set in a tough urban area where dancing is banned, which actor plays the rebellious teenager who challenges this rule? Reflect on where you lived and your favorite recreational activity during this time.

A. Kevin Bacon

B. Patrick Swayze

C. John Travolta

D. Tom Cruise

9. In which film does the character Benjamin Braddock, played by Dustin Hoffman, receive the single-word career advice, "Plastics"? Think about your career or educational journey when you first saw this film.

A. "Midnight Cowboy"

B. "The Graduate"

C. "Rain Man"

D. "Tootsie"

10. "I feel the need - the need for speed!" is a famous line from which iconic 1980s movie?

A. "Dirty Dancing"

B. "The Breakfast Club"

C. "Top Gun"

D. "Footloose"

MULTIPLE CHOICE SOLUTIONS:

1. C. Sgt. Pepper's Lonely Hearts Club Band

Trivia: This album is renowned for its artistic cover and eclectic mix of musical styles, heralding the "album era."

2. C. Neil Armstrong

Trivia: Neil said, "That's one small step for man, one giant leap for mankind," as he stepped onto the lunar surface.

3. B. Color Television

Trivia: The first official broadcast in color was the Tournament of Roses Parade on January 1, 1954.

4. C. Independence Day

Trivia: Also known as the Fourth of July, it's a federal holiday marked by fireworks, parades, and barbecues.

5. B. 1950s

Trivia: Artists like Elvis Presley were instrumental in popularizing this genre, turning it into a cultural phenomenon.

6. C. CD Players

Trivia: The first commercial compact disc player, the Sony CDP-101, was released on October 1, 1982. It provided listeners with a new and innovative way to experience music, offering improved sound quality, durability, and the convenience of direct track access.

7. C. The end of World War I

Trivia: Veterans Day was initially celebrated as Armistice Day, marking the end of World War I at the 11th hour of the 11th day of the 11th month in 1918. It was renamed Veterans Day in 1954 to honor all U.S. veterans.

8. B. The Fall of the Berlin Wall

Trivia: The fall in 1989 symbolized increased freedom and the beginning of the end for the Soviet Union.

9. A. Richard Nixon

Trivia: Although John F. Kennedy set the vision for landing a man on the moon, it was during Richard Nixon's presidency that Apollo 11 achieved the milestone on July 20, 1969.

10. D. Woodstock

Trivia: Woodstock, held in August 1969, attracted an estimated 400,000 attendees. Iconic performances by artists like Jimi Hendrix, Janis Joplin, and Jefferson Airplane made this a legendary event, symbolizing the peace and love ethos of the 1960s counterculture movement.

FILL IN THE BLANKS SOLUTIONS:

1. Marx Brothers

Trivia: This comedic group made 13 feature films, with "Duck Soup" and "A Night at the Opera" among the most famous.

2. Dream

Trivia: Delivered in front of 250,000 people at the Lincoln Memorial in Washington, D.C., this speech is a cornerstone in the fight for civil rights.

3. Sputnik

Trivia: Sputnik's launch began the space age and the U.S.-U.S.S.R space race.

4. Orlando

Trivia: This magical theme park is known globally and continues to be a significant tourist attraction.

5. Cuban Missile Crisis

Trivia: For 13 days, the world was on edge as the U.S. and U.S.S.R. negotiated the removal of Soviet missiles from Cuba.

6. Energy

Trivia: The 1979 energy crisis occurred due to the Iranian Revolution, leading to decreased oil output. It emphasized the U.S.'s dependence on foreign oil, increasing interest in energy conservation and alternative energy sources.

7. Rose Bowl parade

Trivia: This event precedes the annual college football game, attracting millions worldwide viewers.

8. Moscow

Trivia: This boycott was in protest of the Soviet invasion of Afghanistan.

9. Television

Trivia: The television became a household staple in the 1950s, transforming entertainment and news dissemination. Iconic shows like "I Love Lucy," and events like the moon landing were experienced collectively by the nation, establishing television as a central element of American culture and society.

10. The Ed Sullivan Show

Trivia: This show brought iconic acts like Elvis Presley and The Beatles into living rooms across America.

MUSIC AND MOVIE QUIZ SOLUTIONS WITH TRIVIA:

1. **C. "Don't Stop Believin'" by Journey**

Trivia: Released in 1981, this song became one of the top-selling catalog tracks in digital history, showing the enduring love for classic rock anthems.

2. **B. "Say Anything..."**

Trivia: Released in 1989, the boombox scene became one of the most iconic romantic gestures in film history, immortalizing the film and the song "In Your Eyes" by Peter Gabriel.

3. **D. "We Are the Champions" by Queen**

Trivia: Released in 1977, this song became an anthem for victories, especially in the sports world, echoing in stadiums and arenas around the globe.

4. **B. "Saturday Night Fever"**

Trivia: The 1977 film catapulted Travolta to stardom and sparked a disco craze that defined the late 70s.

5. **B. "Forrest Gump"**

Trivia: Released in 1994, this film's unique storytelling and iconic quotes have made it a classic, earning it several Academy Awards.

6. **C. "The Breakfast Club"**

Trivia: "Don't You (Forget About Me)" was performed by the band Simple Minds. Initially, the band was reluctant to record the song, as they felt it didn't fit their style. However, it became one of their biggest hits, reaching the top of the Billboard Hot 100 in the U.S. The song is forever associated with the iconic ending scene of "The Breakfast Club," where the characters leave detention, forever changed by the day's events. The film, directed by John Hughes, became a quintessential teen classic of the 1980s, capturing the struggles and complexities of adolescent life.

7. **C. "Dirty Dancing"**

Trivia: Patrick Swayze's character, Johnny Castle, utters this iconic line to Frances "Baby" Houseman, played by Jennifer Grey, in the beloved 1987 film "Dirty Dancing." This romantic drama dance film became a massive box office hit, known for its memorable lines, passionate dance sequences, and the enduring soundtrack featuring the song "(I've Had) The Time of My Life." The film's themes of young love and overcoming social differences have resonated with audiences for decades.

8. **A. Kevin Bacon**

Trivia: Kevin Bacon starred in the 1984 movie "Footloose" as Ren McCormack, a Chicago teen who moves to a small town where dancing and rock music have been banned. The film's soundtrack, including the title track "Footloose" by Kenny Loggins, became one of the most famous soundtracks of the era, echoing the youth's unyielding spirit and desire for freedom of expression. The movie and its music became synonymous with the vibrant and rebellious energy of the 1980s.

9. **B. "The Graduate"**

Trivia: "The Graduate" (1967) is a pivotal film highlighting the generation gap and the societal changes in the 1960s. Feeling disillusioned and uncertain in post-college life, Benjamin Braddock offers unsolicited career advice to get into the plastics industry, indicating the older generation's focus on material and industrial progress. This film became iconic for portraying young adults' angst and uncertainty facing an established societal structure, amplified by Simon & Garfunkel's evocative soundtrack, including the memorable song "The Sound of Silence."

10. C. "Top Gun"

Trivia: Released in 1986, "Top Gun" starred Tom Cruise as Pete "Maverick" Mitchell. The film was a massive hit and became well known for its action-packed aerial scenes, memorable lines, and the iconic song "Take My Breath Away" by Berlin. The movie's success significantly boosted Navy recruitment and cemented Tom Cruise's status as a Hollywood A-lister.

Made in United States
Troutdale, OR
11/18/2023